Prodigal Son

Book Three of the
Fovean Chronicles Intermission
By
Robert W. Brady, Jr.

A real man is measured in a child's eyes.

The Fovean Chronicles Intermission
Book Three: Prodigal Son
© 2008 by Robert W. Brady, Jr.

ISBN: 978-0-9861961-1-9

This book is a work of fiction. Names, characters, places and incidents are products of the author's imagination or are used factiously. Any resemblance to actual events, locales or persons, living or dead, is entirely coincidental.

Cover art: by Adrijus Guscia

Back Cover: None

First Printing

10   9   8   7   6   5   4   3   2   1

Dedication:

This book is dedicated to the memory of Gertrude R. Lindell.

In the end, we all left you, not because we had to, but because we could.

It isn't something we're proud of.

Known Fovea

Prologue:

When her father's good friends at the Eagle Inn informed her of the handsome warrior with the great, white stallion and expensive Dwarven armor who'd come to stay with them, seeking work as a caravan guard, Aileen had been cautiously optimistic. At nineteen years of age, most of her friends were either married or betrothed, and most of *them* had at least a child on the way.

When she'd met the man named 'Rancor,' her heart melted in her chest for him. Tall as a god, golden hair and blue eyes like her own, with a piercing stare that could melt cold steel and soft hands that her cheek fit into perfectly, that gave her a delicious tingle as they passed through her hair.

He didn't spend countless days complimenting her or telling her of his great deeds, as a Volkhydran would have. She'd never had any taste for the males of her own people, dark and boorish as they were. Rancor amazed her by informing her that he bathed daily and that he'd invented a type of brush that removed the excess food from his teeth after eating. For a man born to kill, with a great sword over his shoulder, he treated her with amazing gentleness, and she'd seen this as meaning only one thing.

He felt the same as she did. He had to. There could be no other explanation – a man who treats a woman with such caring had to be as smitten as she.

So much more bitter, the truth. She gave herself to Rancor, her first and only lover, and he simply took it, not his first time and certainly not his last. She'd dismissed her other suitors and focused all of her attention on him. The daughter of a wealthy brewer pursuing a common guardsman, she'd lowered herself like a camp whore for him, and all he'd really done is to let her.

He worked for another friend of her father's – Myr might be one of the largest cities in Volkhydro, but it was still a small place in terms of its community. When Uman mercenaries attacked the place, Rancor beat their leader in a sword fight and it was decided that the time had come to send out the caravans. She had run to her hero's side, to give him a victor's kiss and then admonish him, as his woman should, for fighting. He'd brushed her off. If ever she had wondered, she knew right then that her love for Rancor would go unrequited.

She'd given herself to the wrong man, and now she had his baby in her belly.

A proud daughter of the god Law, whose children were supposed to save their pleasures for the marriage bed, she'd accepted her fate and seen him leave, sending her brother Tareen with him on a great adventure. It wasn't two months before the first of the guardsmen came back with his arm in a sling and a message for her from Rancor, and by then she was already starting to show.

She'd broken the scribe's seal, running to her room in her father's house, past sniggering servants who knew of her condition and the dark stares from her father who thought he'd raised her better. She'd thrown herself onto her bed like a little girl and read the words from her Rancor, her heart daring to hope.

My dear Aileen,

I am writing you from Kendo to inform you that we were attacked by those Uman mercenaries on the road yesterday. Tareen and I are both fine, though we did lose two horses and this man, Vled, took a nasty hit. There are still thirteen of the mercenaries on the loose somewhere, but we are being careful. We did split the booty from the mercenaries, so Vled and his family should be quite all right.

After I arrive in Volka I must travel on to Trenbon. I cannot guarantee what my life has in store for me after that, but I cannot be selfish and ask you to wait for me for what will most likely be several months, even years.

I am sorry that this was done in a letter. I wish you well and a good man and a huge family – they will be lucky people, all of them.

Best wishes,
Rancor

Best wishes – she read the words over and over. Best wishes – as one would say to a dismissed servant or a distant friend. Her stomach writhed for the child in it – she still succumbed to sickness in the morning from her pregnancy.

What she'd known was coming had come. She'd been a fool, but it wasn't time to be one anymore. He wouldn't have a change of heart. He wouldn't accomplish his mission and return to her. If he even survived it, he'd just keep wandering, keep finding, and of course keep bedding foolish women like Aileen. This one would leave a trail of broken hearts behind him and never be the wiser.

It wasn't that he was cruel, or evil, or a liar. She'd have seen through that in a moment. Rancor simply didn't *see* the women around him. He had his eyes set on the horizon, to some great future that he didn't share with anyone, and the people right there in front of him, helping him, loving him, were just too close and too small for him to notice.

The sole, surviving guardsman from the caravan returned three months later with a wagon, half of their teamsters and her brother Tareen packed in rock salt. They'd been attacked by Confluni National Guard. The little yellow men from the nation to the West always preyed on Volkhydran caravans, moving grains and produce from the Sentalan harvest. She'd stood with her parents as the servants unpacked her brother's body, another group of them already digging a hole in the family graveyard.

"Did you leave his body there?" Aileen had asked the guardsman, Krell.

"Whose, my Lady?" he'd asked her.

"Rancor's."

He snorted. She'd looked at him, still fearing the worst. In her mind, she was wondering if she could make it to the spot and back to her mother's side without risking giving birth on the road.

"Rancor and I survived it," he'd said. "When the time came, he beat them, then we got ourselves to Hydro, and he left us with the money from your father's kegs."

"He *robbed* you?" her father spluttered, prying his eyes off of the box that held his son's remains.

The head teamster, who'd insisted on personally driving the wagon with her brother in it, stepped up and said, "I've thought about that, my lord. He wanted his final wages and I said I couldn't pay him, and then he'd suggested that I give him the money from your beer. I think that maybe he didn't mean all of it, but that was a blooded man with a sword and, big as he was, I just threw him the coin. I'm sorry if I cost you –"

"You cost me," her father growled at him. "You *cost* me – what? I've no son because of this man. I've a daughter no one will ever marry because of this man. If you think you've cost me for the loss of a few coins, then maybe you should look around you."

Her father lamented his lost heir until she provided him with a new one, in the month of War, the year after. The labor had been agony – Rancor had been a giant of a man and she small even among small women. In the end, the mid wife had had to cut her and pull the baby out to save the both of them.

As she lay with her baby in her bed, the servant women having wrapped her hips tight with sheets to give her back her figure and comfort her from her bleeding, the guardsman Krell returned to her, bowing and apologizing, with another sealed letter in his hand. She'd made them all leave her and she'd opened her last communication from her Rancor.

My Dear Aileen,

It is with heavy heart that I write to tell you that I will not, after all, be returning to Volkhydro – at least not in the foreseeable future. I have joined with a group called the Daff Kanaar, and we are bound for other lands, on journeys that will take years.

I wanted to let you know that your brother died a hero's death defending us against what I now know were Confluni National Guard. If not for him, the Confluni would have raided us unawares and I would no longer be alive. In his honor, I killed more than thirty of them; not counting the ones that fought with us that night. I laid waste to their southern guard and, with these friends, exacted a heavy price for their evildoings.

I beg you to find the happiness that I could never have given you, Aileen. It has been months since we parted. This is the first chance that I have had to write. You deserve better, please find it for yourself.

Sincerely
Rancor

She'd almost let herself cry then. Here, she held this man's child in her arms, its mouth pressed to her breast, and he was wishing her someone else's family. Even if she wanted that, the midwife had spoken to her after and informed her that the child, big as a rooster, had done her a good bit of damage inside and, if at all possible, she should avoid having more children.

She'd already made that decision. Lesser nobles and the sons of tribal chiefs in her own nation had come sniffing around her when the word spread that her father had no son, but she wouldn't have them. Now there was a male to inherit the family business, and she'd done her duty as a daughter.

She was done with it. She'd folded up the letter and hidden it in her pillow case with the other one. Later, when she was up and walking, she'd move them to her secret box – the one with a lock of Rancor's hair that he never knew she'd taken – for her to open on those days when she didn't know how she'd make it to the next.

The god Law punished His daughters severely, who ignored His tenets.

***

In the region called Fovea, where her nation was one of six that survived on Tren Bay, War was a month and, like any month, was named after a god of the same name. The 'War Months,' which began with the month of War and ended with the month of 'Life,' is when countries fought each other. For decades before her birth, that had been a yearly occurrence, but become more rare since the race known as the Uman-Chi, powerful spell casters who never grew old, had created the Fovean High Council to regulate the Fovean nations and prevent war.

But now the nation called 'Dorkan,' had actually attacked both the Dwarves to the north and the Uman-Chi on their Silent Island, and the High Council had called for the sack of the Dorkan city, called 'Katarran.' Volkhydro had sent her sons in an army of almost 2,000 to uphold their honor, the guardsman Krell among them.

Krell had returned in the month of Order and informed her of what he'd seen.

Bouncing her son, whom she'd named 'Eric,' on his knee in nothing but his cloth diaper, he'd told her, "I saw him there as plain as day, a mercenary himself now working for Eldador. I saw him in his armor walk up to the gates of Katarran, and break them with a blow of his hand."

"Certainly not!" she'd said, her son gurgling happily on Krell's knee.

Krell looked away and then back to her. "Well, in fact, my lady, there's rumor as he's fallen in with an Andaron witch named Shela."

"What?" Her heart constricted in her breast. She didn't want to know this.

"Witches, them as aren't wizards, and the ones from Andaron are strong," Krell had told her. He'd been a mercenary himself for years and seen a good part of Fovea. "This one is strong among them, and many say it was her magic as broke the gates and opened up the city. But Rancor is calling himself 'Lupus' now, and he's tied up with a group called the Daff Kanaar, mercenaries for hire no different than the ones I saw him kill here and on the road. But even if I didn't know the man, and now I think I don't, I'd know the horse, the sword and the armor. That was your Rancor."

He took Eric in his huge, rough hands and turned him around to look into the child's face. Then he looked into Aileen's eyes, and handed him back to her. Her Rancor had written to her of his joining the *Daff Kanaar* – in Uman that meant 'Free Legion.' It isn't a name that anyone else would pick.

"We all know whose this one is," Krell said, "but for the path he's on, I'd forget this boy's father, my lady."

"That one fooled us all."

For years after, Aileen heard the troubadours singing of the warrior Lupus and his woman, Shela. Lupus the warrior who'd beaten the Dorkans at the sack of Katarran. Lupus the mercenary who came to Volkhydran cities to buy out the crimes of those who would serve in his army. Earl Rancor Mordetur, of Thera, the new favorite of the Eldadorian King.

Then Lupus the Conqueror, who'd charged ten thousand Confluni at the Battle of Tamaran Glen to save his Andaron slave girl, Shela.

That one broke what was left of her heart.

While the warrior became a legend, and the Earl a Duke, and then the Heir to the throne of Eldador, Aileen raised their son, Eric, in the traditions of the god Law, to be a true son of Volkhydro. She loved that boy with everything in her. Many said that Aileen's tiny body held a heart so great that no bull could bear it. When her father passed and she took over the running of his business, she spent coin to make sure that the boy learned his letters and his numbers, as well as how to be frugal with a copper and generous with a sword in his hand.

When finally all of Eldador wasn't big enough for Lupus the Conqueror, and he sent his armies north to Volkhydro and attacked Volkha, its capitol, Aileen sent that good son south with a sword in his hand, one of Count Tezzen's two thousand warriors, to defend the land she loved from the man she loved.

The day she left, she prayed to Law for the son, and to War for the man, that somehow both of them should remain alive, and neither have to bear the awful burden of fighting the other in a field of battle. She pledged her life and her soul, if only the gods could return either or both of them to her.

Aileen loved that son, but she'd never forgotten the man who gave him to her. She'd followed the man's story for almost half of her life.

However this is the story of the son.

Chapter One:

A Boy to a Man

"So you broke your sword, and you come to me with this toy?" Count Tezzen of Myr challenged the boy.

Eric straightened. Yes, he'd broken his own sword, searching for the body of a Swamp Devil on the field of the Battle of the Foveans, as this last battle was called by the troubadours. No, the one that he'd found to replace it was *not* a toy.

As any Volkhydran warrior would, he pulled the blade. He'd been insulted.

Better to be dead.

Tezzen's eyes widened. "You'd match me?" he asked.

On a marshalling field east of Medya, where the Myr Regulars had made camp, come late to the battle, longhaired, shaggy Volkhydrans took note of a boy squaring off on a man. Who among them hadn't done the same? The point wasn't that you might be beaten. The point was that you'd better have the courage to fight the Volkhydran who dared to insult you.

At sixteen years of age, Eric was no different.

He took his new sword two-handed and placed his feet apart. He'd trained with Tezzen since he could hold a blade – his mother, Aileen, had insisted on it. There were certain habits of his that *felt right*, as he put it, and Tezzen detested them.

This was one.

"I think I'm finally going to beat that bad habit out of you," Tezzen informed him, pulling his own blade, *Blood Drinker*, from over his shoulder.

Tezzen stood five feet eight inches, average for the race of Men. He'd been a warrior all of his life, developing the pronounced arms and slender abdomen of a swordsman. He didn't wear much armor – sleeves and greaves, as the Volkhydrans liked to say – protecting his arms and legs. His body he kept bare.

Eric wore a chain mail shirt that hung down to his knees, a steel cap and, of course, his sword – the black blade, four feet long, with the intricate basket that he'd found on the battle field. His blond hair flowed past his shoulders, his blue eyes focused on his opponent's hips, his fair skin already flushed. He *loved* to fight – to match his sword against others. Now, he felt, he had a blade worthy of him.

At over five feet tall, he was exceptionally large for his age, but then he'd been told that his father was a towering giant. Personally, he'd never met the man.

Tezzen chopped for his shoulder with Blood Drinker, turning his wrist at the last moment and then pulling back for a stab at the heart. A lethal blow, Eric parried as his own surprise registered. His trainer, his Count, his master had just tried to kill him. No one had ever done that before.

So be it.

He swung low, pulled the blow and then curved high, aiming for the jowl. When Tezzen avoided the first blow and moved to parry with the second, Eric tapped the blade aside and spun completely around to deliver a full-force chop for the side, a meeting of blade-for-blade, the victor to be the stronger of the two Men.

Tezzen's blade shattered on impact. Eric barely managed to pull the blow and leave a red line across the other man's middle.

As he'd been trained, he spun the weapon one handed on his right and seated it at the other man's throat.

"Yield?" he demanded, barely breathing hard. The victory had come far too easily. Blood Drinker might be an old blade, but it was forged of Volkhydran steel and should not have shattered.

"I'll never yield to a common," Tezzen began.

Before he even thought about it, Eric took his blood price of the man, pressing the blade, cutting the skin at the Count's jaw line.

One part of him asked him how he *dared* to do this to the Count of his own city, but a larger part insisted that he'd won, and that he deserved the prize.

"Your submission or your head," Eric informed the other man. "I'd be happy to see a new Count of Myr."

Tezzen's eyes widened. He'd aged over forty, a gaffer by some standards. Eric wondered if he'd realized that before now.

"I yield, then, young Eric," Tezzen informed him, moving his left foot, ready to step back away from the blade.

"You meant to say, 'Your Excellence,' I think," Eric informed him. 'Where was this coming from?' that rational part of his brain demanded of him. Tezzen was his Count. Of course, he could knight anyone he wanted, but to *demand* it at the point of a sword?

The other part of his brain insisted, 'Why not? You've beaten the man – collect the spoils!'

In southern Eldador, Angadorians had Knights – warriors who rode in Duke Stowe's personal guard. In Volkhydro there were chiefs and sub-chiefs to the west, against the Confluni border. Dukes and Earls ruled what were considered the more 'civilized' cities of Volkhydro to the east. Counts and Viscounts held the land under them. A Viscount – little more than a common, a little less than a noble – is legally endowed to hold land, have vassals and collect taxes, but subordinate to their Counts, their Dukes and their Earls in defense of Volkhydro.

"I yield, then, your Excellence," Tezzen nodded, and stepped away from the weapon. "I think that I won't doubt you while you hold *that* sword, but if you're going to be one of *my* men, then remember that you're holding it for me."

Eric touched his new sword's pommel to his brow and said, "Ever in your service, then, my lord," then sheathed it bloody.

He'd done it! Sir Eric of Myr – a Viscount of Volkhydro! His mother would be glowing with her pride for him. The family business would excel with the lesser tax burden and the ability to collect serfs as laborers. As other Volkhydrans clapped him on his back, Tezzen pulled a rag from his sleeve and wiped at the blood on his neck.

"I used to think I taught you too well," he said, "but I think that maybe I didn't teach you anything at all, Sir Eric. Your father is the only man I've ever seen take that stance, but then, he couldn't beat me with it, like you did."

"You knew my father?" Eric asked him. All of his life, he'd heard of his father only as some caravan guard who'd bedded his mother, then run off on her. Sweet, loving Aileen, the daughter of a brewer, had raised him with no less pride than any other mother, but never spoke to him of his sire.

"I was one of many who trained him," Tezzen said. "As my man, you know, I can have no secrets from you. Come to my tent tonight, and we'll celebrate your ascendancy and plan war strategy, and I'll tell you a few things your mother should have."

Eric's mind swam. "Of course, my lord," he said.

That night, Tezzen held a feast for his warriors. Eric had heard rumors that their King had abandoned Hydro and moved his army to Vol. Soon they'd do the same and prevent the Eldadorian Emperor from rolling up the river.

Viscounts, Earls, barons and squires sat at the count's table, Eric sat among them with his new sword over his shoulder. Ale and venison roved up and down the table, Eric taking his fill of both.

He'd hoped for a private audience with the Count, but that didn't seem likely.

"Looks to me," Tezzen was informing a warrior next to him, a friend of his own family named 'Krell,' "like Hydro will suffer Volkha's fate. The Emperor's army is too large, and if his son can defeat the Hero of Tamara, then Dragor of Hydro has no chance."

Eric had heard of this. Karl Henekhson, who had fought alongside of the Emperor at the Battle of Tamaran Glen, had faced and been defeated by the Emperor's son, Vulpe, at the city of Medya. What made the loss even more humiliating was that 25,000 Eldadorians had met nearly 100,000 from all over Fovea. If Eldador could assure victory at those odds, then who in their right mind would face them?

"No one can beat Lupus the Conqueror," Krell said, referring to the Emperor. "You know that he made an appearance at that battle, with 4,000 Theran Lancers? No. The best thing that we can do is to weather this storm and make the rest of Volkhydro so expensive to invade that the Emperor looks elsewhere."

Eric didn't like hearing that. He'd been born a Volkhydran and, in his heart, he knew his people were invincible. It couldn't be a matter of being defeated. It had to be a matter of bad leadership allowing this to happen.

"Has there been any sign of the Daff Kanaar?" another Volkhydran, a bushy-haired baron with one eye, asked. His beard was greasy from venison and wet from ale.

Tezzen shook his head. "No, thank Law," he said. "Supposedly the Daff Kanaar have taken the city of Kattaran in the Emperor's name and renamed it Luparran, right on Dorkan soil. If the Daff Kanaar are just keeping the Dorkan army from helping the rest of Fovea to fight against the Emperor, then we're really in a fix."

The Daff Kanaar had made an appearance on Fovea at about the same time as Eric's birth. They recruited criminals and disgraced warriors from all over Fovea, gave them a uniform and a wage and a new opportunity to live their lives. Supposedly you entered the service of the Daff Kanaar with any name you wanted, and what was on your back, and no questions were asked. You were called 'Daff Kanaar' and nothing else mattered other than the job you did.

Lupus the Conqueror had been a founding member of the Daff Kanaar and still wore their emblem on his breast – a hook symbol with a dot over it. Lupus' was black. Other founding members had other colors. Every nation on Fovea had at one time or another employed the Daff Kanaar either to attack for them or to defend them against the ambitions of their neighbors. The Daff Kanaar, as the largest mercenary force on Fovea, had become fantastically wealthy.

When they fought they almost always won and no one wanted to face them on the battlefield. It went without saying that no one wanted to be caught between them and the Eldadorians.

"If the Dorkans aren't going to help us, then we'll have nothing at our sides by Uman," another warrior said, and slammed his hand down on the table where they feasted. "Who the hell wants to fight alongside o' damn Uman?"

Uman made up another of the races on Fovea. They were built like Men, but thinner, slighter, with fairer skin and pointed, lobeless ears. They lived as much as three times as long as a Man, but they weren't the fierce fighters that Men were. Uman were more concerned with enlightenment and nature.

Someone had told Eric once that Uman might be the abundant mortar that held the rare stones of Men into a castle called 'civilization,' but that was the sort of crazy thing that an Uman would say, and Eric disregarded it.

He didn't want to fight alongside Uman, either.

The warriors would continue arguing into the night. He retired early with the party still raging. Let them eat and drink, he thought to himself. Let them pat each other on the backs and think that they would muddle through.

That wasn't the Volkhydran way, it wasn't *his* way and, by Law, his chosen god, he wouldn't have it!

"My lord?" someone said behind him.

He turned to find a squire of the Count's court. As a Viscount now, these people answered to him. He nodded to the squire and said, "I am Sir Eric."

"Yes, my lord," the squire said. He was a dark and smallish fellow, in the brown livery of a Volkhydran court. "I've a message for you, from your home city."

Eric raised an eyebrow. "And that is?" he demanded.

The man looked down, then back up into Eric's eyes. "I fear," he said, "that your mother, Aileen, calls for you from her death bed."

Chapter Two:

His Father's Son

The ride from Medya to Myr took ten days – Eric arrived sore and travel worn, his horses little better.   After the rout of the Andarons at the Battle of the Foveans, horses had become plentiful in Volkhydro, and Eric had used his new-found status to collect a string of four. He traded off between them as he rode.

His family brewery had been built within the walls of Myr, but to the south, away from the city's western gate and eastern wharves. Tezzen had joked many times that, if anyone every invaded Myr, then at least they wouldn't find the warriors sober.

The unshod horses' hooves clopped on the cobblestones outside of the low walls around his family residence.   The brewery with its vats and wells and storage bins for hops and barley lay to one side of the cast iron gates, stretching for more than the lengths of 100 horses. To his left, the family manor had been built of hearty stones from the north, the windows with solid oak shutters bound in black steel, the double doors massive and banded in copper atop the steps to the main entrance. Eric leapt from his horse, handing his reins to an older man, a retired warrior who'd served the family since he'd lost an eye in battle. The other looked him up and down quizzically.

"War's left you different, young Eric," he said, the reins in one hand, his other pushing back a mop of long, brown hair from his good eye. In the string, the horses hung their heads down, exhausted. "Ye've lost weight and gained muscle, and I see ye've got yerself some spoils."

"Few enough of those," he said. "Our army was beaten. The Eldadorian Emperor has the capitol, has Medya, and probably has Hydro by now as well. Gharf Bendenson is pulling our troops back to Vol."

The servant – Eric recalled his name as Dramor – shook his head. "Our King is too generous with his land and too greedy with his soldiers."

"And his gold," Eric said. "He still isn't paying regulars. The cities support him with their own money.

"How's my mother?"

Dramor looked to the manor, up at the window where Aileen often sat, watching to the south. "She lives," he said. "You've come in time, or I wouldn't be keeping you.

"Eric," he said, and laid his free hand on the boy's shoulder, "if ever there was a woman with little joy in life, it's your mother. I've known her a long time, and she's too young for this dying. You've got to get her up, get her moving, give her something to be on about in life."

Eric nodded. "Well, Tezzen declared me a Viscount in Myr," he said. "That might lift her spirits."

Dramor laughed, then coughed and put the back of his free hand to his mouth. "I think what she'd like instead is a few bouncing babies around."

Eric blushed. He'd always stood out as a blond in a sea of dark-haired men, and blue-eyed among those of brown, so he'd had his share of attention from girls. Remembering what had happened to his mother had always made him afraid of following in his father's footsteps.

"If need be," he said, looking back up to the window. "Somehow, I don't think that what mother needs are more bastards here."

Dramor sent him on his way with a pat on the back. Eric pulled the chainmail shirt over his head once inside of the doors. He left it and his cap for a servant, then climbed the stairs two-at-a-time to get to his mother's room. He found her there with a Volkhydran serving woman named Trice. A gray-haired, toothless widow who cleaned for them, Trice was as much a mother to the family as Aileen. She ran to Eric and hugged him.

"Oh, look how you've growed in a month," she informed him, running from his mother's bed to take him in her arms. Then she held him at arm's length.

"But not *eaten*! I'll make you a good stew, by Law, and get the fat coming back on you. Here, you sit with your mother – she's in and out, but maybe you'll get some energy back in 'er."

"What wrong with her, Trice?" Eric demanded. In her bed, piled with comforters on such a hot day, she looked flushed, her thick blond hair laid out on her pillow, as if Trice was already practicing arranging her for her coffin.

Trice shook her head, her turtle-mouth puckering and her eyes rimming. "No one knows," she said. "Not the healers, not the priest of Law when he came by. Your mother's soul is leaving 'er, Eric. It's almost like it… just has somewhere else to go."

She pushed herself away from Eric and fled the room. Eric moved as quietly as his hard-soled boots would let him to the sunlit side of her bed, and sat by her hip, fishing her hand out from under the comforters. It should have been warm, but it chilled him instead, her delicate fingers cold as death in his hand.

She stirred. "Mother?" he whispered to her.

Her eyes fluttered open, as blue as his, but rheumy. Eric immediately recognized what Trice had been talking about. She looked for all the world like someone whose body had died and now waited for the soul to follow.

"Eric?" she said, squinting into his face. Then she recognized him and smiled, closing her eyes again. "Eric, my boy. You've come to see me off."

"Off, mother?" he asked her. "Off where? Where are you going?"

"Off to be with *him*, of course," she told him. "I see him now, in his shiny armor, and his great sword. He's on his stallion. It's so grand! After so many years, he's finally come for me."

Eric leaned forward. He could smell the herbs on her breath - the ones that healers used to induce sleep. He'd needed them once after a particularly bad fall when learning to ride. They could bring strange dreams.

"Him, mother? Who do you see?"

She opened her eyes and looked into his, suddenly seeming to be focused. "Why, your father, Eric," she said. "I told you. He's come for me. I'm finally going to be with him again."

Eric's heart froze. "Father's dead, mother," he said.

Sometimes the spirits of loved ones whispered to the dying to lure them into the next life. Eric took one look around the room, as if expecting to see one of them now, creeping over the edge of the bed.

Aileen shook her head. "No, son," she said. "I'm sorry I had to tell you that, but I didn't want your father coming back, just because his honor forced him. I always knew he'd come back to me, but I wanted you to be a surprise to him, not a burden."

Eric straightened. His father, still alive? Tezzen had said just ten days ago that he knew the man. Could the whole city share a lie and keep it up for him for his entire *life*?

"My father?" was all he could say.

She tried to turn in her sheets, but sighed and closed her eyes and said, "Reach into my pillow, son."

He slipped his hand inside the soft, warm case for her pillow and withdrew an old leather scroll tube. Eric recognized the Dwarvish symbols on its sides. The fat that had been used to seal one end had soaked into it and darkened the leather long ago. Eric turned it upside down and two scrolls of parchment, each tied with a faded yellow ribbon, dropped out onto the bed.

"I had that scroll tube brought to me from the Silent Isle, where the Uman-Chi live," she informed him. She reached out a hand and stroked the side of it.

The Uman-Chi were a hybrid race of Uman and a dead race called the Cheyak. Thousands of years past, the Cheyak ruled all of Fovea, but fell. The Uman-Chi had tried since then to replace them, and lived on what was called 'The Silent Isle,' an island in the middle of Tren Bay, in a city called 'Outpost IX.'

"He had it when I met him. He threw it aside when he was done," Aileen said. "A courtier picked it up and sold it to a merchant, who sold it to one of our shippers, who thought that I might want it."

Eric shook his head. This wasn't the story that he'd heard about his father. What would have brought him to the Silent Isle? What was he doing with a Dwarvish message tube?

"Read them," she told him.

Eric unrolled the first scroll – he recognized the flowing letters of a professional scribe. It wasn't uncommon for men not to know their letters, and to pay others to write for them. The guard for a caravan would be such a man.

It was a good-bye letter that called her, "My Dear Aileen." Something about being attacked, and how the writer had to go to Kendo, then to Trenbon, and then he'd never see her again. It was signed, "Rancor."

Eric dropped the letter and looked into his mother's face, her eyes closed. He only knew of one Man who had that name.

Impossible!

He snatched up the other scroll and pulled off the ribbon.

"He's so handsome," his mother said. "Rancor, I forgive you, my darling. Look at your strong son! Doesn't he look just like you?"

She reached for him from under the covers.

"Rancor, I prayed and prayed – I knew you'd both be in battle. I prayed you wouldn't meet. I offered up my life to War and Law, if only would both come back safe."

She continued her murmuring. Eric read the second letter, written by a different hand, more cribbed, perhaps a scribe, but not a Volkhydran – someone who didn't normally write in that language.

If the first letter had left him with any doubts at all, the second one would have answered them. Here he boasted of joining with the Daff Kanaar and smashed her dream of his ever coming home. He bragged of killing Confluni for her brother. He begged her to find happiness – *happiness!* – without him.

She deserves better, he closed, and then his name again, "Rancor."

She deserved better.

Better than *the Emperor of Eldador*! For the love of Law, his father was Lupus the Conqueror, and his latest goal was the Volkhydran nation!

He turned his attention back to his mother, and saw her head turned to one side, her mouth puckered in a kiss, her chest still. He waited for it to rise, but it never did, and it never would.

Trice entered the room, took one look at them and dropped the tray she'd been carrying, the ceramic bowl smashing on the hard wood floor, brown stew and chunks of meat and carrots flying everywhere. She put her hands to her mouth, the tears already flowing down her cheeks.

Aileen of Myr was dead.

Eric buried his mother in the family cemetery, outside of the walls of Myr, in a stand of trees where the family cemetery kept her fathers and theirs going back for hundreds of years.

Eric ordered her headstone to read:

Aileen
Born in the 59th year of the Fovean High Council
Died in the 96th
Taken from us too soon
No sweeter soul has ever walked amongst us

The priest of Law gave her a eulogy. Eric really didn't listen to it. Dramor, Trice and the rest of the staff all wept appropriately. A fellow Volkhydran named Aleg, a common like he had been, but a man very learned of numbers, had informed him that the brewery had been losing money for years and that the family fortune was seriously depleted.

Eric wasn't stupid. The false news came as the vanguard to an offer to buy him out at a fraction of what he knew the place was worth. Aileen had insisted that Eric be schooled in his numbers as well as his letters, and she'd always taken a strong hand in the business.

Eric walked away from the grave site. He'd hung his new sword over his shoulder but dressed in black cloth pants and tunic to symbolize his mourning. Aleg informed him, "I grieve for you, Sir Eric, but I've gone back to the other merchants in Myr, and in other cities, and everyone is very excited about doing business with Eldador. That's good for the people of our land, but not for its businesses."

"We shouldn't be *doing* business with Eldador. We should be *killing* Eldadorians as we find them," he said, through gritted teeth. Beside him, Dramor nodded.

Aleg nodded solemnly. "As well we should. Yet Hydro fell while you were returning here and has even been renamed to 'Hydrus.' Our capitol city is now 'Lupha,' and both are declared for Eldador. We don't control our own coastline any more, Eric. Even if we wanted to fight, how could we afford it?"

'Even if we wanted to,' Eric repeated in his mind. He seemed almost to be counseled now by that part of him that had let itself be known when he had squared off on Tezzen, and then demanded he be elevated. Since he'd found this sword, he'd found a newer, angrier, more aggressive part of his brain, and it wasn't shy with its opinions.

'Since when,' it asked him, 'did a Volkhydran not want to fight to defend Volkhydro?'

From thought to action, Eric ripped the sword from its sheath and had its keen edge at Aleg's throat.

"Do you think I'm a fool?" he demanded.

"M-m-my lord, Eric, please, you're distressed..." Aleg's eyes held a contemptible fear.

Eric's eyes met the coward's across the blade. "Distressed? You haven't *seen* distressed. But if you try to cheat me, what you *have* seen is your last breath."

"My offer..." he said. Eric pressed the blade.

"Thousands of warriors new to Volkhydro, the Emperor dying to do business with us, and you say that this is a bad time to be selling *beer?*"

Eric shoved the man with his free hand. He fell on his behind, a scattering of papers flying out from under his arm. The bastard had brought the deeds with him, ready to sign.

Eric had wanted to simplify things by keeping a chastised and better educated Aleg on, but to dishonor his mother like this? That wasn't the Volkhydran way.

Eric's sword pinned the man to the ground, via his heart. He coughed a spout of blood and died before them.

"Never liked that one, anyways," Trice commented.

Killing another common would usually bring out Tezzen's warriors, looking for justice or at least a bribe. Eric *was* one of those warriors now. No one would come looking for him.

"Throw him in the river?" Dramor asked.

"Leave him for the crows," Eric said, and yanked his blade free, then wiped the end on dead Aleg's trousers.

"The man had a family," Dramor reminded him.

"So do the crows."

***

One of his grandfather's best friends had always been a shipper named Bawser. Eric sought him out after leaving Aleg.

"Yes," he admitted, from behind his desk, in his office in his yards, where he could look out one window and make sure that everyone was working. A life spent behind a desk had made Bawser a heavy-set, jowly man with no hair on his head and plenty on his fingers and forearms. His brown eyes spoke of a shrewdness that his body denied. "I knew your father. The man worked for me, in fact, when he met your mother."

Eric's blood boiled. Bawser must have seen that, too, because he pulled a cudgel out from under the desk and laid it on its surface, between them.

"Think to settle some imagined score with me, young Eric," he said, "and you'll get a rap from that. I said I kept the lie. I didn't create it. That was your own grandfather's idea."

"Why?" Eric demanded.

"Well, at first," Bawser said, and leaned back, but not so far that he couldn't still reach the weapon, "because of the shame of it. Law's daughters don't give themselves before the marriage ceremony. The man was a common guard."

Eric had dealt with that his whole life. "And then?"

"And then," Bawser informed him, and leaned forward, looking right into Eric's eyes, "we knew your father first as a mercenary known for his ruthlessness, then as a noble known for his greed, and finally as an Emperor known for his hunger. Why, young Eric, would we want to make you a target of *his*?"

"The love for him killed my mother," Eric said, simply.

"Like as it did," Bawser nodded, sitting back. "Like as everyone knew it would, too. You've never met your father, Eric, I have. He was a leader and a champion. He still is. You knew - you looked at him and you just *knew* that he on the road for something grand."

"Grand," Eric repeated.

"I offered him my business, if he'd settle down here with your mother," Bawser informed him, "but he left anyway. Now the son has come to me instead. What do you want me to offer you, to settle you down?"

Eric looked him in the eye. He could forget this now that he knew the truth. He could let it lay. He could just be Eric - a young and wealthy man with a very bright future.

But that wasn't the Volkhydran way. He'd be damned if it would suffice for the son of Lupus the Conqueror.

"Run my mother's business for a while," he said, "or have someone you trust do it. I already had to plant one man who tried to cheat me."

Bawser smiled wide. "I never liked Aleg," he said, "and I knew he was up to something. Yes, that's wise, Eric. That's smart. Yes, I'll help you run that business – we've got good market..."

But Eric was already shaking his head. "Not help me, Bawser. Do it for me. Not forever. Just for a while."

"And what will you be doing," Bawser asked him, "for 'a while'?"

That other side of Eric's brain perked up again, and he put a hand on the pommel of his new sword.

"I think I need to meet a man," he said.

Chapter Three:

The Gathering Dark

Eric didn't leave Myr in the mad rush he'd been in when coming there. It proved a simple matter to let Bawser put a man in charge of the family business. Eric as the owner of a successful brewery could take coin and food for himself, pack three of the horses that he'd brought north and then go south without too much thought. He could even have brought a few warriors, but he didn't want that. He didn't want to share in what he had to do.

He carried his mother's letters in their leather tube, in his tunic against his breast. He'd read them both one hundred times already. He knew every letter, every phrase and every tear stain on the edges.

Years of his mother never really being happy, years of her being almost there with him, molding him but never really taking him into her arms, ran through Eric's mind now. People told him that a widow sometimes had these thoughts, but how much worse, a used woman?

No, he reminded himself at every cook fire, on every ride as he travelled south through Volkhydro toward the port city of Hydrus. Within a week he started to pass the refugees, the displaced Volkhydrans who wouldn't be Eldadorians. He passed more than he cared to see but fewer than he'd hoped. People trudged along with packs on their horses, on their wagons and on their backs, looking to restart their upended lives with whatever they could carry. Some managed to drive a few aurochs – the huge bovines, barely tamed, that could either pull, give milk or provide meat.

He saw his mother's face on the daughters and the women. He heard her voice in their complaining and their sorrow. Eric found himself growing darker with every mile south, his bile swelling in his heart. Oddly, this new portion of his brain seemed almost to be talking to him.

Justifying his right to vengeance and amplifying his pain, it led him to camp alone, even when there were others around. When he needed food or simply saw the opportunity, he hunted alone, packing his own meat and stretching his own furs. If others needed him, he simply ignored them, or stared them off until they went away.

Now and again he'd come across a camp of women who travelled alone. He knew these, as well. In any invasion, the spoils of the war eventually fell to taking the women of the defeated. Eric knew the ravaged faces. He'd seen the way they bowed their necks, looked sideways at him and held their bellies. They could move sometimes and pass themselves off as orphaned women, unless of course they carried the bastards of the victors. Then they could have terrible lives as street walkers, low servants or the women of low men. Until then they'd camp together and console each other, waiting for their bloody time or, not having it, try to plan out something of a life.

Some would go to midwives if they could find them, and try to kill their unborn children. If caught, these were considered the lowest women of all.

Eric passed by one group and rode close to them. They looked up in fear. It wasn't uncommon for less honorable men to take their pleasure with these women, justifying their actions with the thought that whatever damage had already been done.

This happened on the 25th of Destruction's month. Eric had been born on this day. It was his 16th birthday. Thinking that he'd never spend this or another one with his mother had placed him in a dark mood.

He threw the women a handful of silver. They looked from him, then to the coins, then back to him.

"What do you want for this?" one asked.

She must have already guessed her fate.

Eric shook his head. "It's yours," he said. "Do what you will.

"Try not to kill your baby," he added, then turned his horse and rode off.

***

It wasn't until the 3rd of Chaos that he came across something that he couldn't ignore.

He'd just topped a rise, moving south a day's ride from Hydrus. He'd been planning his strategy – he'd represent himself as what he was, a Viscount of Myr, come to meet the Emperor. He'd make a big fuss if they tried to take his sword. It wasn't uncommon for nobles to meet armed, after all. He'd get within range of the Emperor, and then he'd read his letters aloud for the world to hear.

That angry part of his brain was telling him that he'd come up with a stupid idea – that the Emperor was too clever for this, that he wouldn't care about the letters. Eric couldn't imagine anyone not reacting to what had been done to his mother.

Instead, from the top of the rise, he looked down on a battle between three warriors and a child.

The warriors were Volkhydrans, from the Volkha side of his nation, long-haired and dressed in furs, armed with heavy swords. The child stood alone, a short sword in his hand, his back to his horse. He'd probably tried to mount and ride. The bodies around him attested to the savage fight that had gone on – ten warriors of the race of Men and Uman in Eldadorian livery, at least a dozen Volkhydrans.

He kicked his horse in the ribs, dropping his string of the other two. He ripped his sword out of its sheath on his shoulder.

The horse leapt down the ridge. One of the Volkhydrans turned and saw him, giving a whoop for the other two. One of them, he knew, could hold the boy while the other two addressed him.

Eric didn't know what had happened here and, in fact, he didn't care. The boy was an innocent, like Eric's mother, and Eric had drawn his sword on Volkhydrans before. They should allow the boy to yield or, even better, to ride. These men had no honor and Eric had no trouble fighting them.

The Andaron horse had likely seen combat before. Andarons were a race of Men - fighters like his own people. With his sword in his right hand, Eric took the horse's reins in his left and leaned to his right, reaching out with the blade, pretending to come in low, then planning to swing high for the enemy's arms, to disable them, unless their swords were too long. In that case he'd use his momentum to break their weapons from their hands and then take them on the return pass.

Likely they'd just go after the boy, but then it would be him armed.

Eric swooped in. One of the Volkhydrans stood his ground, one other ran for the other side of his horse. The third held the boy as Eric had expected.

Eric turned the horse and went for the running man – if he could take him from behind, Eric could kill one and focus on the other. The first man tried to move in for a shot at his horse. The running man turned.

Eric engaged, his sword longer than the other warrior's, but his reach shorter. He went for the weapon, hammering down on the blade as he passed.

Once again, the other weapon shattered. Shards of steel flew into the unmounted man's eyes. The one who'd been running charged his horse. The beast reared, then turned, Eric clinging to the reins, as the third man spun around with his sword drawn.

That was a mistake. The boy struck, his weapon springing from the Volkhydrans rib cage. The horse dropped and Eric chopped down at the second man's head, crashing through the Volkhydran's sword, then through his unprotected head, blood and brains flying.

Eric tugged his weapon free and turned his horse to find one man running, holding his eyes, his sword forgotten, and two dead on the ground, the boy grinning up at him with a red blade.

***

Eric took the opportunity to actually examine the boy he'd saved. He looked to be around twelve, brown hair and eyes and a strong jaw. He'd come heavily armored, which is what probably kept him alive. His helmet lay on the ground next to him. He wore his hair close to his scalp. The boy met his eyes like any man would. Someone had spent time raising him properly.

He clearly wasn't Volkhydran or Andaron – and he didn't have a Confluni's yellow skin and slanted eyes. Somehow, he doubted that a Dorkan could afford such heavy armor for a child.

"You're an Eldadorian?" Eric demanded of him, breathing hard.

"I am," the boy said. His voice was soft, steady, almost musical. It didn't tremble like a child's.

"You're kind of small for the Regulars," Eric commented, "and pretty young for the Wolf Soldiers."

"You don't know who I am?" the boy asked, seeming incredulous.

"No."

"Then why did you save me?"

"Well," Eric said, and looked over his shoulder at the running man. His two other horses were cropping grass nearby – he needed to get them before they got it into their heads that they could have their freedom. "I could call that one back, if you can't bear saving."

The boy smiled. He sheathed his sword, spattering its metal sheath with blood from his enemy, and extended his hand up to Eric. They took each other's wrists. Eric felt the blade of a dagger in the boy's sleeve.

"I'm called 'Chewee,'" the boy said. "Short for Agtani Chewla."

"An Andaron?" Eric was skeptical, releasing the boy's wrist. He had the olive skin, but anyone campaigning could tan. "No Andaron wears armor like that, and that's an Eldadorian war horse."

"That it is," Chewee admitted. "I'm from one of those families that moved to Eldador. My father is a Wolf Soldier."

"No Wolf Soldier has armor like that, either," Eric said, looking in the boy's eyes.

"Spoils of war," Chewee said simply, and shrugged.

Eric sighed. "I don't suppose this Wolf Soldier father of yours is anywhere near," he asked Chewee.

"Well, I have a home to go to, if that's what you mean," Chewee informed Eric.

"I've business in this area," Eric said. "If it's close, then I'll take you. You'll likely see more of their kind around."

Chewee nodded and mounted his horse. He took a look at the bodies, then at the hills around him. "Does this place have a name?" he asked.

"I assume it does," Eric said, "but I don't know it."

"I'd like to find my way back here," Chewee said. "These men were friends of mine."

"You being a Regular, and the son of a Wolf Soldier," Eric said, and kicked his horse into a trot.

Chewee kicked his own horse after him. The two on the tether raised their heads and saw him. Eric saw the stance – they were going to bolt, and it was going to take forever to catch them.

Chewee saw it too, and pulled his horse off to the right, starting a wide circle around the two horses. Eric raised his eyebrows in appreciation. The boy had Andaron training if nothing else. He kept up a trot to the horses, who started right into Chewee's path. The boy's horse leapt forward and he reached out impossibly far from his saddle, snatching up the tether between the horses and deftly wrapping it up on his saddle horn. Faster than Eric would have thought possible, the boy had the two horses under control.

Chewee returned with the horses in tow, a huge smile on his young face. Eric just shook his head.

"We're off then?" Chewee asked.

Chapter Four:

Reunion – of a Sort

The boy wasn't a complainer, Eric gave him that, and he knew his horses. Chewee seemed content to pull the string behind him when Eric's arm grew tired. He rode light and fast in the saddle and, for the armor he wore, he could actually swap horses without dismounting. Eric tried it and nearly broke a leg.

Chewee saw to the horses before himself when they stopped, knowing that he could be borne if he was sick or tired, but the horse needed to be healthy to carry him. They pushed east without the complaining that Eric would have expected of a young boy.

Like Volkhydrans, Eldadorians measured distance in 'daheer,' ten daheeri being the distance to the horizon on the flat plains. After travelling a few, Chewee started humming to himself. Eric had done the same – sometimes the quiet of the road, with no other sound but the horses' hooves, weighed on him. Eric recognized an old tune about the Hero of Tamaran Glen – the Volkhydran warrior named Karl, son of Henekh, who'd turned a battle for the Emperor when he'd still been a Duke.

The song had two parts: a background refrain of, "He fights, he fights, he'd have gone all night;" and then the main part which described the battle. Eric grinned and started humming the refrain, catching Chewee's attention.

"Do you know the song?" he asked.

"I think everyone knows *that* one," Eric answered.

"Would you like to hear it? You can sing the refrain."

"Oh, I don't really sing."

"Do your best," Chewee said, and then cleared his throat and looked out toward the horizon.

He opened his mouth and sang the first words, *"Alone in a forest, hungry and tired, his first time to stray from his father's strong arm."*

Eric immediately felt his mind swept away by the boy's voice. Chewee's singing skill took Eric completely by surprise. His voice carried Eric through the journey Karl had made with a few thousand Daff Kanaari warriors and one hundred Wolf Soldiers, through the battle and it's turning, to Karl's victory in the name of Lupus, who became the Conqueror after that battle. Eric saw it all in his mind for the first time. The clash of swords, the press of the Confluni – Eric experienced it as if he where a ghost, the whole thing swirling around him.

Eric actually had to take a moment to calm himself down after Chewee finished. He'd never reacted to a story like that before – he'd never heard anyone who could sing with such amazing skill.

"You forgot to sing," Chewee said, finally.

"Wh – what?"

"The refrain," Chewee said. "You didn't sing it. It's better with the refrain."

"I, um – oh," Eric was at a loss. Beneath him, even his horse had slowed, seeming more content for having heard the song.

"Chewee – that was amazing," he said, finally. "I've never heard – I mean – are you the son of a troubadour or some great operatic?"

Chewee just smiled. "No," he said, "I'm pretty much just me. I learned to sing at my nanny's knee. She always encouraged me."

A nanny? No one had nannies. In Volkhydro, even if a woman died in child birth, as many did, a man would take another wife or invite some relative to raise his child. The very wealthy prided themselves on their children – who would trust them to another?

"Andarons have nannies?"

Chewee looked for a moment like he'd been caught in a lie. Perhaps he had, Eric thought. Young boys were notorious liars. Eric had been one himself. Once he'd told the hands around the brewery that this was his second life, and he'd been a powerful sorcerer before, and spent a week trying to cast a spell. Some of the older ones remembered that still.

But Chewee would say no more on it, and Eric let it lie. Finally night fell and they made camp near a stand of trees and scrub, where the horses could graze and water ran close, but far enough not to threaten flooding them. Eric pulled out his own bedroll while Chewee offered to get wood for a fire.

"I wouldn't do that," Eric said. "Eldadorian patrols will be out. I'd hate to have to justify why I'm moving toward the city."

Chewee grinned, then caught himself. Eric wondered at that. Personally he dreaded meeting his first patrol. The Emperor's had a reputation for ruthlessly defending what he took and his warriors were renowned killers. Who knew *how* they were treating Volkhydrans in conquered territory?

Chewee rode with his head up, actually looking for someone else. Perhaps the boy romanticized the great Lupus the Conqueror, Eric wondered.

Eric had no such imaginings.

"I think we'll be safe," Chewee said, but Eric shook his head.

"It's warm," he said. "There are no animals to worry about in these hills. Let's not risk it. I jerked some venison two days ago and that will feed us."

Chewee shrugged and pulled his saddle from his horse, then his saddle blanket, laying them down traveler's style, where he could lay on the one and pillow his head on the other. Eric normally didn't like to lay the saddle or the blanket on the ground for fear of it getting dirt or insects in it, but there was nothing either to hang them on or suspend them from here.

Perhaps a low-hanging branch, he wondered. He took a few steps closer to the trees in the waning light. One of them must have a low-hanging branch. He slung the saddle over his shoulder and started toward the stand.

"Eric, don't move," Chewee told him. His voice took on a whole other tone, authoritative like a full grown man. Eric obeyed before he even thought about the strange order, then turned his head back to the boy.

Chewee was up on his feet, his brown eyes searching the stand, leaning forward as if he were hunting. After a moment, he straightened, and he said something in a language that Eric didn't know and had never heard before.

To his utter surprise, something in the stand answered him. It was a light, trilling voice, almost singing. Eric was reminded of the boy's song suddenly. There were qualities that rang the same.

"Eric," Chewee said, as one might speak to a horse that needed calming. "Someone's going to come out of that stand. She's a friend of mine, but she's armed, and I don't want you to fight her or threaten her in any way."

Eric dropped the saddle and the blanket. Chewee immediately took a step towards him, his hands raised palms out, calling something back to the stand in that same language.

"That's exactly what you don't want to do," Chewee said. "This friend of mine is very protective of me, and if she thinks for a moment that you'll hurt me, she will kill you before you can even think of defending yourself."

"I'm not just going to – " Eric began, but Chewee shook his head.

"I owe you my life, Eric," he said. "On mine, no harm will come to you, but please, just don't move."

Eric sighed and nodded. He turned back to the stand, and Chewee called out again in that strange language. This time, a woman stepped out from the trees, as if she had been one of them herself. She wasn't as tall as he, willowy, dressed in leather pants and a halter, with daggers on her upper arms and thighs. Most striking was her purple hair and, as she came closer, her exquisite gray eyes.

An Aschire, Eric knew from his lessons. They lived in a forest also called 'The Aschire,' pocketed between Eldador and Andaron. By and large, they lived there, they died there and they never left their forest, with two exceptions.

They loved the Emperor and would do anything to support him. He'd called them out by the thousands many times to help him to defend his country, and once in an invasion of Outpost IX, the capitol of the Trenboni nation in the Silent Isle.

The Emperor's nanny, his children's personal guard, was an Aschire named Nina. Troubadours sang of her reputation for her brutal loyalty to Lupus and his children, and had nick-names like 'The Emperor's Watch Bitch,' 'The Emperor's Other Wife,' and 'Mistress of Pain.'

The Aschire were deadly archers, and this one had a bow in her hand and a quiver of arrows over her shoulder.

There could be only one reason why she was here, now.

"Vulpe, who is this?" she asked Chewee, never taking her eyes off of him. He forced himself to relax, not giving her a reason to nock that arrow.

Eric knew that name. Every Volkhydran knew that name now. Vulpe Mordetur, the son of the Emperor, Lord High Commander of the Eldadorian Regulars.

Eric had come looking for his father, and instead he'd found his half brother.

Chapter Five:

One Way In

Nina of the Aschire had come pacing out of the darkness like some predatory cat, her eyes searching his, searching the terrain around him, looking for the ambush, ready for the trap. Once she'd cleared the stand of trees, others followed her, a command of Eldadorian Regulars one hundred strong. How they could have moved so many so quietly was beyond Eric. No nattering band of Volkhydrans could have done it.

But then, no nattering band of Volkhydrans would have let themselves be led by a woman, either – especially not an Aschire.

With the sun already set, they made a base camp and lit a fire. One hundred Eldadorian Regulars coordinated their efforts and created what they called a 'jess doonar,' Uman for 'Small City,' with an earthen wall, a row of tents, pickets for their horses and scattered fires where the warriors cooked or often just sat staring. The warriors broke apart into teams, the teams clearly knew what they had to do. A guard schedule had been posted and already four warriors marched the periphery with shield and sword ready faster than a gang of Volkhydrans could have agreed that this was a good place to stop.

Nina reclined at a fire with Vulpe and Eric, one of the soldiers turning a deer on a spit over a fire for them. There were three other such cook fires. She kept staring at Eric, looking into his eyes whenever she could. When he spoke to her, sometimes he felt his skin tingle for no reason.

"So you've come to see what's going on in your nation," Nina repeated for the third time, "and, if possible to meet with the Emperor."

Eric sighed. "Yes," he said – again. "I'm a Viscount of Myr, under Count Tezzen, and I want to know the Emperor's plans."

Every time he said, this, she shook her head and Chewee – Vulpe – broke out in a big smile. He liked the boy, but he was getting tired of this.

"What?" he demanded.

"Well, you're lying," she said, simply. "You're *not* here just to meet the Emperor -"

She stopped when his hand flew to the pommel of his sword.

"You're calling me a liar?"

Several of the Eldadorian warriors, as well as Nina and Vulpe, straightened. Putting hand to sword this close to Lupus' son – his *other* son – was probably something they took seriously, he reasoned.

However, they *had* let the boy get out of their sight, too. Vulpe had gone off with only ten warriors to do some scouting on his own – something that he wasn't supposed to do, apparently - and something *certainly* beneath the stature of the Lord High Commander of the Eldadorian Regulars. Nina had been searching for him ever since, and had picked up his trail yesterday. What had been a one-day excursion for him now had taken three, and she was on her way back to Hydrus – the renamed city of Hydro – with her charge.

"Yes," Nina said, looking him right in the eyes. "You're a liar, Eric of Myr. I've cast my spell on you and seen it – you're lying about what you want to do."

He was up on his feet, she no slower. Ten of the Eldadorian Regulars, a mix of Men and Uman – one a Volkhydran – stepped forward, but she put a hand up and stopped them. Vulpe remained seated, watching from the fire, interested but not interfering.

"A woman with arms is responsible for her words, Nina," Eric informed her, and pulled his weapon.

Faster than he would have thought possible, she had a dagger out of each arm sheath and leapt for him, impossibly high, her heel lancing out for his jaw. Eric actually felt the air move across his cheek as he pulled his upper body to one side and raised his sword two-handed to take her in the leg as she passed.

She trapped his weapon between her daggers and tried to twist it out of his grasp, almost succeeding. Tezzen had taught Eric the value of a loose grip, and the handle merely turned as he held it. Nina landed on her feet and Eric pulled his weapon from her daggers, holding the handle high over his head, the blade pointed down between them.

That stopped her cold. She looked quickly at Vulpe, then back at Eric, her eyes narrowed. Tezzen had told him that this was an unconventional move, one that put him off balance, however the Count had never gotten past it, either. Eric relied on his unusual height and strength for his age to be able to spin the sword one hundred eighty degrees for a downward chop that had all of his weight behind it. He'd splintered shields and practice swords with it many times.

"Where did you learn that?" she demanded of him.

"Ask your god when you meet him," Eric spat back, and spun his wrist. The black blade hammered down at Nina's unprotected head. She met it with her two daggers, making an 'X' of them before her to trap his blade. This time the weapons shattered, barely stopping him.

She gave a shout of alarm as the weapon cleaved down on her torso. Once again, impossibly fast for anything that walks on two legs to move, the Aschire lurched backwards, the weapon barely touching her breastbone, parting her leather halter.

Her pert breasts bobbed free. The look of rage that crossed her face as she dropped a shattered dagger to either side actually made Eric hesitate, even more than the sight of a half-naked woman for the hormonal boy. Rather than pulling her other two daggers, she raised a hand between them, white with power.

Magic! She'd known he was lying because she'd cast a spell on him. Volkhydrans had few wizards, and Eric didn't like or trust magic. He certainly didn't want it used on him without his knowledge.

"Stop!" Vulpe commanded.

All heads turned to the Prince.

"He dies," Nina spat, her chest heaving. A thin trickle of blood already ran from her breastbone to her waist.

"If not for him, I'd have died," Vulpe said, looking up at her. Now more than half the camp circled them. Eric noted that they kept their distance from Nina.

She had a reputation as one of Lupus' most ruthless servants – that there was *nothing* she wouldn't do to protect his children.

"How do you know he didn't send those warriors himself?" Nina demanded of him.

"Did you?" Vulpe asked, looking into Eric's eyes.

"Of course not," Eric spat, insulted just to be asked.

"I don't need a spell to tell me that he's not lying now," Vulpe said, turning to Nina. Already, the white light that had engulfed her hand had dissipated. "He saved me, Nina. You aren't using your magic on him just because he has a strong forearm."

Nina's upper lip curled. She tossed her purple hair over her left shoulder and reached for the two halves of her halter, holding them together between her breasts with one hand. Without another word, she left the circle, the Eldadorian soldiers parting for her without a word as others went back to their duties or their rest. Eric just stood there with his sword drawn, wondering what had happened.

"Sit, please," Vulpe said, holding his hand out to the spot next to him.

Now that he wasn't pretending to be 'Chewee,' Eric saw a whole other side to Vulpe. Here sat the twelve-year-old who'd outfoxed his Volkhydran King and then the united Fovean armies in two battles on Volkhydran soil. If he'd taken Hydro then he had three cities to his name on this campaign – more than most generals five times his age. Supposedly, when bounty hunters had kidnapped his mother and sisters, he'd raised a small band of Wolf Soldiers and Theran Lancers and taken them back in an ambush on the ambush that those bounty hunters had laid for him.

Vulpe had distinguished himself as a military genius perhaps even greater than his father. Eric sat down next to his half-brother, wondering for a moment what *he* had inherited from the Emperor of Eldador.

"Where did you learn to fight like that?" Vulpe asked him. The Eldadorian soldier had returned to turning the carcass over the cook fire. His inattention had let it burn a little on one side.

"Count Tezzen," Eric began, but Vulpe shook his head.

"No Fovean taught you to stand with your sword like that," he said. "Nina saw it, and so did I. There's only one man who fights that way, and that's my father. I tried to learn to do it and I couldn't. The weight of the sword pulls me over front-ways. But you use it just like he does for one, powerful blow that crushes your enemy before you.

"If you fight like my father and you've never met him, I'd like to know how you learned it."

Eric looked into the fire. "Tezzen actually tried to train that and a few moves like it out of me," he said. He shook his head, "I don't know, Chewee, it just… feels right to fight that way. I know it isn't going to pull me over. I know that it's going to protect me and give me power."

Eric looked to his right, at the boy reclining on a hide next to him. Vulpe's eyes seemed more cunning to Eric now that he knew Chewee's true identity. This boy had led the life that *he*, Eric, should have had as the eldest son of the most powerful man on Fovea.

Eric's mother should have lived in comfort and security and Chewee, if he had ever been born at all, should have had the forever-sad woman with a secret that burned out her soul and left her like a husk more than a person.

"Those are ill looks," Vulpe noted. The soldier turning the game on the spit pulled a dagger from his belt and cut a huge slab from the hind, catching it on a wooden plate. He held that against his middle and portioned it out three ways, then stabbed one of the three pieces and held it out to Vulpe.

Eric almost took it out of habit, and he couldn't help thinking that Vulpe had noted that. He smiled and pulled his own belt dagger, taking the meat from the soldier, who stabbed a second piece for Eric.

"Give him two," Vulpe ordered him. The Eldadorian soldier, an Uman with fair skin, looking ruddy in the fire light, shot a questioning look, but simply stabbed through the first piece into the second.

He held the dagger out to Eric, the Volkhydran pulled his own belt knife and traded it from the Eldadorian's. He looked at Vulpe but didn't eat.

"Bring it to her," Vulpe told him.

"What?"

"Nina," Vulpe said. "You don't know her like I do. She holds a grudge. She won't accept being beaten by you, and she's going to do everything that she can to get even. You bring her that, you make your peace with her."

"Maybe I should just - " Eric began, but Vulpe held up his hand.

"She'd run you down," Vulpe said, knowing what he had in mind. "You go and she'll decide that she was right. You'll never see it coming."

Eric nodded. He stood with the two slabs of venison on the soldier's dagger and walked to the tent where Nina had gone. He felt like every set of eyes in the camp was on him as he scratched at the tent flap.

"What?"

She didn't sound happy. Vulpe knew this woman. "I've brought you food," he said, for lack of anything else.

He heard her sigh. She likely knew what he was doing. Women thought this way. "Can you sew?" she asked, still from inside.

"What?"

She sighed again. "Get in here," she said. He could hear her moving in the tent.

He entered. The tent was plain – a bed roll, an oil lantern hanging from the center post, a sack with her possessions in it. Nina was sitting cross-legged opposite the tent flap, waiting for him, her top still off. Her breasts were as small as a young girl's, complimenting her willowy frame. The scratch between them still bled, an ugly gash on her breast bone. She had a needle and thread in her hand.

Eric laid the meat down, still on its dagger and steaming. "You can't get that, can you?" he asked.

"No," she admitted. "And there isn't another woman around."

"Give it here," he said. He'd stitched his share of warriors before. Children did this job in Volkhydro to get them used to wounds and keep from tying up the adults from fighting. Usually an old gaffer of gammy oversaw them. These were skills that would carry them through their lives.

Like now.

She handed him the needle and thread. He held his palm out and said, "Lick my hand."

"What?" the scowl on her face was telling.

"Would you rather I rub my own spit on you?" he asked her.

She sighed.

"I've got water, you idiot," she informed him, "and alcohol." She pulled a rag from her leather sack and a water skin from behind her. She wiped herself down, then pulled her legs underneath her and arched her back, pushing her long purple hair behind her shoulders and raising her hands behind her head.

"Be quick," she said, and then looked him in the eye, "and keep your manners."

Eric smiled a half-smile and said nothing. He started at the top and teased the right side of the laceration with the end of the needle until he got a good spot, then drove the needle through it, under the gash and up through the other side.

She hissed but said nothing. He did what his people called a 'butterfly stitch,' crossing the stitches to make a good, tight seam that would leave very little scarring.

"Can't you just - I don't know – magic this?" he asked her, after he had a few stitches in.

"I can't do that on myself," she said.

He looked in her gray eyes – he'd never seen that color before – then back to his job. "Really?"

"Stop that."

"What?"

She sighed again. "Stop showing off your eyes," she said. "Yes. They're perfect."

He chuckled and started another suture. "I was thinking that about yours."

"Oh."

"Do all Aschire have gray eyes?" he asked her.

"No," she said. "Just me and my father."

"I have my mother's eyes," he said. "My father's too, I suppose."

"You don't know?"

Yes, he thought, he did know, but he wasn't telling his Watch Bitch. He made his second-to-the-last suture and then said, "He left before I was born."

"Oh," she said. She'd relaxed, he noticed. To one side, their meat cooled, still on the dagger. He started the last suture, and she added, "My – ow! – my mother did the same."

"Died in child birth?" he asked. She shook her head.

"Just left one day," Nina said. "Very rare for an Aschire – she's the only other one of my people to leave the Aschire for a different life, as far as I know. My father claims that I'm just like her."

Without thinking, he leaned forward to bite the string off close to her skin, where he'd tied it. She gasped as he ended up rubbing his cheek and eyelid on her nipple. He felt her hand in his long, blond hair before he could pull away.

He straightened as she pulled his head away, spitting out the string. "Sorry," he said. "That's how you break the string."

"You didn't hurt me," she said, then looked down and smiled.

Looking back up at him she added, "Well, other than the ways you hurt me, of course."

"I apologize for that," he said, finally. He reached for the dagger. "Are you hungry?"

She pulled a dagger from her thigh sheath and said, "He's a bastard, you know."

Eric had been called that before – many times. He hated that term. It made him feel dirty – like he'd done something wrong. "What?"

"Vulpe," she said, prying her slab of meat from his. "He sent you in here because he knew I couldn't stitch that myself."

"Oh," Eric said, and took a bite so that he wouldn't have to say more.

"He does things like that," she said, and took a nibble. She still hadn't put her top on. "He's no different from his father. He likes everyone around him to behave in a certain way, then he uses them."

"Oh?" Eric raised an eyebrow. She nodded.

"He must have something special planned for you."

"And how do you know that?" he asked, taking another bite.

"Well," she said, "he's a Mordetur, of the House Mordetur, son of Rancor Mordetur, Emperor of Eldador, and you're alive, aren't you?"

Eric nodded, still chewing. Kind of hard to argue with that.

It made him wonder what sort of Mordetur *he* would be.

Chapter Six:

Off to the East

They didn't bother his string of horses. They didn't try to take his sword. He would have put up a fight if they had – a man doesn't part with his steel. Eric rode behind the Prince and next to Nina, her halter stitched together with a piece of rawhide and her sternum crossed with travel bandages. She seemed to have no trouble keeping her seat, but her gray eyes looked adamantly forward, telling Eric that she fought the pain.

A strong woman, he informed himself. He'd eaten with her, he'd mended her. She'd tried to kill him.

He smiled to himself – some Volkhydrans would consider them engaged.

This was it, though, he told himself. This answered all of the questions. This put him face-to-face not only with the Emperor, but with the Imperial family.

Then he could do anything he wanted to.

They'd trot for most of an hour, then they'd rest for about ten minutes, then ride again. The horses, Andarons, Eldadorians and Angadorians, were inexhaustible, the warriors grim-faced and quiet.

Usually a few would roam out to each point of the compass, giving them a wide view of the terrain.

Vulpe didn't want to be ambushed again.

They'd become an army of occupation, with their main strength in Hydrus. During rests he picked up snatches of conversation.

The city had fallen after a tough fight, street-to-street. They still have twenty-five thousand warriors here, another five in Medya, where Lupus had begun a massive reconstruction. People had seen Dwarves come down out of the mountains.

Eric's King, Garth, was still holed up in Vol. A lot of people wanted to go wrap him up and push up the Llorando. No one had ever gotten past Hydrus. The Llorando stopped them when the Volkhydrans couldn't. The river made a sound like a man weeping on this side, like a woman on the other. Spending too much time listening to either sent a person into a deep depression. The cities on this side were built where they were because, for whatever reason, they were immune to the sound.

It really bothered Eric that his King had turned out a coward. An army of Volkhydrans, bravely led, would destroy any army. The Emperor had his reputation, but Volkhydrans had nearly one thousand years' history of destroying all enemies.

Finally they came to the end of the long day. They could see the hills that surrounded Hydrus, and the path through those hills. Vulpe clearly wanted to push through and enter the city late, however a newly-taken city needed to be approached more cautiously. Tezzen had taught Eric many times that beaten and defeated were two different states of mind.

"We'll camp," he informed them. "Build the jess doonar and set the watch. Lieutenant, I don't want to forage this close to the city. Break out our rations. Nina!"

"Your Highness," she said, pulling her saddle from her horse. Eric was doing the same.

"Can you reach my mother?"

Nina dropped the saddle into a pile with the rest, then lowered her head. Eric dropped his next to hers, on his blanket. There was simply nowhere to hang it. These people knew nothing about horses, or they just didn't care.

"I have her," she said, finally. The soldiers were already digging the earthen mounds and constructing the tents that would form their little city. "She's relieved to hear that you're alright. They've been hunting down and killing raiders for a week – your father has gone north with 1,000 Theran Lancers to make a point to Bendenson."

Vulpe nodded. "Let her know we're up with first light," he said. "No need to risk the horses this close to home."

Nina nodded. "She wants to ride out to meet you, but she really can't leave the city." Nina paused, and then smiled. "I know that frame of mind. She'll be up and mounted before the sun."

Vulpe gave a little laugh. "Tell her I love her and I'll see her soon."

He turned away from Nina and was back among the warriors. The Man he'd addressed as his lieutenant followed him, repeating his order. Eric saw the lieutenant - probably twenty years Vulpe's senior - following the boy's commands as almost comical.

Nina stepped up next to Eric. He needed to check her stitches anyway. It would be a miracle if they hadn't torn.

"He's changed so much this year," she commented. "He'll have his 13th birthday soon. He should be playing with toys, not making war."

Eric shook his head. The privileged son of the Emperor would have no sympathy from him. Eric didn't find himself hating Vulpe, but he wasn't going to be weeping for the hardships in his life, either.

Not after what his mother had gone through raising him.

"We all grow up as we need to," he said, cryptically. He turned and looked the girl in her eyes. "We all need to mend, too. I have to check your stitches."

"You want to get my top off again, you mean," she grinned back at him. He straightened. That sounded like a comment on his honor.

"They're itching," she added, noting his posture, no doubt. "Do you have more alcohol?"

He nodded. Everyone carried a little, just in case.

"Put up my tent and I'll let you have at them," she informed him.

"I'm doing you favors to do you favors now?" he asked her, raising an eyebrow.

She looked after Vulpe, making herself keep her gray eyes off of him. Her purple hair framed her face.

"I'll let you know when you're doing me favors," she told him. "Meanwhile, I'll bring you your meat tonight."

He built her tent for her, and his right next to it. An Eldadorian soldier showed him where. He laid down his bedroll and then hers, and hung her lantern. He'd brought his own medical kit in a pouch on his belt. She entered just as he was finishing.

She nodded, frowning. He turned his back to the rear of the tent and sat, facing the flap where she had sat. She sat facing him, her knees touching his, a leather pouch in her hand.

"Hard tack," she said, and offered him the bag.

He took it, pulling the drawstrings open. She watched him, something going on in her gray eyes, still easy to see even in the dim light. It was summer and the sun had just set, but there was a glow in the air regardless.

Inside he found strips of cured beef – hard tack perfect for the trail. He pulled out a long piece and offered it to her.

She opened her mouth, keeping her hands in her lap. He chuckled. Sure – he could feed her. He had very little experience with women - certainly none with Aschire - but if this was how they behaved, so be it.

He put the end in her mouth, she took it in her teeth. "Take the other end," she told him, looking in his eyes.

"What?"

"Take the other end in your teeth," she said. Already a little drool collected at the corner of her mouth.

"Trust me."

He shrugged, leaned forward and took the other end of the strip of beef. She pulled back from him, looking in his eyes, grinning.

The tug-of-war went on for only a few seconds, then with a flash before him, her dagger parted the beef. He blinked with surprise, pulling back from the weapon, watching her hold the cut beef in her teeth.

He almost spit it out, but he didn't know if that would be rude or not, so he took it in his mouth and chewed it. She did the same. "Ever done that before?" she asked him.

"No," he admitted. The beef was tangy and lightly salted. The idea was to chew it until it was almost a paste in one's mouth, then suck the juice out of it and swallow the rest. It would fill a person's stomach and leave plenty of energy for the day's travel.

"Good," she said, and reached into the pouch for another piece. She apparently didn't intend to feed him her whole meal. He was still working on his first piece and she popped in the second.

"How bad are you itching?" he asked her.

"It's not bad," she said. She reached behind her neck, under her hair, and untied her halter, exposing her breasts for him again. Next she reached behind her back and untied the wrapping that held her bandages in place, dropping them.

The stitches had pulled a little. One hung too loose. Her skin was healing in a fine red line, a little redness in the skin around it. He reached into his kit and pulled out a clean, white rag and a vial of alcohol.

"You do it," she said to him.

He shrugged. "I'd like to redo one of those stitches," he said, "but you'll have a worse scar. It isn't bleeding. I'll squeeze it and see if there's pus."

"Ok."

He put some alcohol on the rag and wiped around the edges of her wound. He couldn't avoid contact with her breasts and nipples. She just watched him, chewing her hard tack, not reacting to the alcohol. He knew from personal experience how much that could hurt.

Finally he put the rag aside and put his hands on her midriff, his thumbs under her breasts. He looked her once in the eyes, then pushed on the wound gently. He didn't want to reopen the wound, but he needed to force out any infection.

He found none. He creeped his thumbs up a little higher and a little lower – nothing. "It looks clean to me," he said.

She nodded as he took his hand away. She reached into the pouch, fished out a piece of hard tack and said, "Open your mouth."

"You're going to feed me now?"

"You have alcohol on your hands," she said. "I don't want to eat it."

"It's clean."

"Are you hungry or not?" she insisted.

He shrugged and opened his mouth. She fed him and, a little while later, she fed him another piece. They sat in the dark, her topless, chewing, until the meat was gone.

"Are you going to sleep?" she asked him.

He nodded. "That ride took it out of me," he admitted. "I'll dress your bandages - "

"I can do it," she said, cutting him off.

"I don't mind," Eric said. "You should let the air get to it tonight, though."

"If I'm going to sleep like that, I'll need a bodyguard," she informed him, smiling.

He sighed. "I can sleep outside your tent, if you want," he offered. "It's a warm night."

Her smile faded.

"Never mind," she informed him.

"What?"

"Nothing," she said, not looking at him. "I'm tired – you'll come back in the morning?"

"Do you want me to –" he began.

"Fine," she said.

He shrugged. He pushed past her to get out. He felt her hand touch the side of his face and his shoulder as he passed her.

Emerging from the tent, he saw Vulpe watching the tent mouth, eating from his own leather bag. "Is she well?" he asked.

Eric nodded, then looked back at the tent mouth, and then at Vulpe. He felt like he was missing something, but he didn't really know what.

Vulpe shook his head and smiled. "Go to sleep, Eric," he said. "Tomorrow is another day."

"She wants me to wrap her in the morning," he informed the Prince for some reason.

Vulpe nodded. "I'd think she would."

Chapter Seven:

In the City of Hydrus

They woke with the dawn, and Eric found Nina with her tent already packed and her dressing already in place. His own disappointment surprised him, as if she were someone he took care of.

"We'll eat in the saddle," she informed him as, all around them, the Eldadorians were leveling and dismantling their jess doonar. "Shela has already left Hydrus, and we'd like to actually meet her on the road."

Eric nodded. His own tent was easy enough to knock down and pack on one of his spare horses. He retrieved his saddle from where he left it and commenced to beat the blanket clean.

"What are you doing?" Vulpe asked him, Nina right behind him.

"The dirt and twigs aren't good for their hides," Eric informed him. He stepped back out of a small cloud of dust that he'd made. "It's better to keep a clean blanket."

Vulpe looked over his shoulder at Nina, who shrugged. "Mother never said anything to me about that," he informed them.

"Does she beat out her saddle blanket?"

"She does," Nina said. "The Emperor, too – I never asked them why."

"You should hang your saddle if you can, and the blanket over it to dry," he informed them, as his own groomsman had informed *him* years before. "Keeps everything fresh and clean."

"You still pick their hooves?" Vulpe asked him.

Eric nodded. "Before and after I ride."

"Why after?" Nina had picked up her own blanket and was beating it in the air like his. A cloud of dust flew from it.

"You can pick up a pebble from the road as you ride, and put your horse up fine, just to find him lame in the morning," Vulpe informed her. "There's other things, too – the hoof rotting disease they can get from standing in their own urine –"

"White line," Eric said. "Not much of a threat on the road, unless they step in the droppings of another horse, and you don't pick out their hooves."

"I never pick my horse's hooves," Nina admitted.

"I know," Vulpe said. "I've been doing it for you since we've left. Mother would switch you if she saw your horse's hooves like I found them."

She smiled. The thought caught Eric as funny, too. She caught him, and doubling up her hands, she swung her blanket at him like a club.

"Hey!" he protested, dodging her first swing and then, on the follow up, catching the blanket in mid-air. He pulled her close to him, her stomach against his, her gray eyes looking into his.

"If you pull those stitches *I'll* switch you," he warned her.

"Promises," she said, so close to his face that he could feel her breath on him. She pushed away from him, snatched the saddle and ran to her own horse.

Vulpe sighed and shook his head. Together they saddled their own horses and cleaned their hooves, Nina keeping to herself, occasionally checking on them over her shoulder.

Most of the camp was ready to leave by the time they mounted. The lieutenant informed Vulpe that he planned to remain with twenty stragglers to clean out the camp, and that they'd catch up within two hours. Vulpe nodded and gave a whistle, putting his thumb and forefinger between his lips. "Head out!" he shouted.

He put his heels to his mount's ribs and the horse picked up a trot, the rest of the hundred falling in smartly behind him. He sent five riders to each point of the compass once again, this time much closer because the hills limited their vision. It wasn't even half an hour before they identified the beginnings of a road, more a trail, to Hydrus.

Eric kept to the back this time. Nina ranged to the north with the Eldadorian scouts there. A fellow Volkhydran, a soldier in the Regulars, hung back with him.

"You're Eric of Myr," the Volkhydran informed him.

Eric nodded. "I am."

"Aileen's son," he pressed. Eric just nodded.

"I'm Tamoor, of Myr," he said. "My father worked for your mother for years, until the Count pushed up his taxes, and he left for Eldador."

Eric knew about that – the Count wanted to raise levies for an invasion of Sental and he needed more gold. He tried to tell the Volkhydrans that they'd make the money back in loot, but most didn't believe it.

"Taxes go up, not down," Tamoor said. "Give me Eldador, where the taxes are always the same, no matter what happens, and you can know tomorrow how much of your own silver you'll have."

Eric looked the older boy in the eye. He had a thin beard where Eric still was only sprouting his whiskers, and long hair kept back in a braid. The Emperor, he knew, preferred to tie his long hair back in a pony tail, and a lot of Men did that now.

Eric left his loose under his steel cap. "Small price to pay for your heritage, then?" he asked.

Tamoor shrugged and said nothing. To their north, Nina kicked her horse and took off for the east.

"You fought with that one, and stitched her up after?" Tamoor asked him.

"Yep," Eric said. He was still fuming over how easily Tamoor had dismissed Volkhydro.

Tamoor shook his head. His brown eyes twinkled with his amusement. "You're a lucky bastard," he said.

Eric's hand flew to the pommel of his sword before he even thought of it.

"A *what*?"

"Hey!" Tamoor warned. "No fighting in the Regulars."

"I'm not *in* the Regulars," Eric informed him, "and you'll take back that comment or I'll carve it out of you."

That angry part of Eric's brain, which had sat quiet for a while, was raging now. *Take him,* it informed him, *and the others will fall in line.*

Fall in line to kill him, Eric thought, but Tamoor put his hands up, palm facing him, showing that he wasn't taking up his sword. "My apologies," he said. "I just meant that Nina doesn't usually leave anyone who challenges her alive."

Eric took his hand off of his sword and put it on his hip, keeping his reins in his left hand and riding. For a moment, it looked like Tamoor was going to move ahead in the line, but then Eric asked him, "Why is that?"

"About Nina?"

"Yeah."

Eric noted that Tamoor made sure that he knew where the Aschire was before he answered, "Well, they don't call her 'Mistress of Pain,' for nothing. You know she's a witch, right?"

"She tried to use it on me," Eric informed him. Tamoor nodded.

"Right – heard about that," he said. "But you're the one stitched her."

"She can't use it on herself, I guess," Eric informed her. Tamoor laughed.

"What?" Eric demanded.

"You're a Volkhydran," he said.

"What of it?" Eric was about to put his hand back on his sword. He'd heard before, 'One Volkhydran is a soldier, two a brawl, three an army and four a war.' He wasn't doing well with his countryman. Eldador had made him strange.

"Think about that – what does the magic care, who she uses it on, herself included?"

"I don't know anything about magic," Eric informed him, and left his hand on his hip.

"I didn't either," he said. "Our people don't fight like that. But I can tell you, I saw that girl take an arrow in the arm, and she pulled it out and swore about it, and then she fixed the hole in her arm and went on fighting."

Eric looked sideways at him. "On your honor?"

"On my life," Tamoor swore.

That didn't sit well with Eric.

Nina came trotting back from the East, just as the warriors they'd left behind ran in from the West. Vulpe halted his troops, one hundred of them called a 'Century,' as beside Nina he saw another woman.

She was dark-haired, olive-skinned, obviously an Andaron. She sat an Andaron stallion, taller in the saddle than Nina, dressed in a black leather halter and skirt with a short-sleeved, black leather jacket with long tails, her hair free over her shoulders. She kicked her horse into a canter the moment she saw Vulpe and ran like she was a part of her horse.

"Empress Shela Mordetur, Mother of the Realm," Tamoor informed Eric, as if he needed to.

Her exceptional beauty was the talk of Fovea, and Eric saw that it wasn't exaggerated. Eric's own heart swelled for her, even as he realized that *this* was the woman whom his father had left his mother for.

The woman who had made him a bastard, with her witch powers and her beauty.

Vulpe trotted out from the main army, most of the soldiers smiling now, probably also overwhelmed with her. She dead-stopped the stallion only feet from her son's horse, then walked it up alongside of his and hugged him in the saddle, pressing her lips to his forehead.

They spoke softly, the urgency easy to hear in her voice. She looked several times at Nina, and Eric threw a glance at Tamoor, who caught it and smiled.

"She's convinced that the only reason the Emperor is alive is because she looks over him," Tamoor said, "so it isn't uncommon for him to campaign, and for her to find a reason to follow. So when her son went out alone, she pitched a fit and sent us out to find him. Little did we know you'd already rescued him."

"So, normally – " Eric began, and Tamoor cut him off with a nod.

"Normally Nina goes wherever Vulpe goes, now that his sister is a powerful sorceress herself and needs no guarding. The Mordeturs are all the same, though. They like to do things themselves, and they like to do them when the mood strikes. Drove his mother about crazy."

"Eric!" Eric heard his name called. He nodded to Tamoor and he pulled his string along after him, trotting up to Vulpe, who'd shouted for him. "Your Highness," he said, when he came within their earshot. "Your Majesty," he inclined his head to the most powerful woman in Fovea, the sweat running in rivulets down her breasts and midriff.

"Sir Eric, of Myr," she said to him, her hand still on her son's thigh, her horse next to him. "I'm informed that you've saved my son's life, and you've come to meet my husband on behalf of Myr."

"Yes, my Lady," he said. He lowered his head and shot a glance at Vulpe, who seemed to be just watching this with no expression.

"Of course, you understand that I can't give you free access to the Emperor, just on your word," she said. He straightened, searching her eyes, trying to see if she meant to offer some offense. She kept on talking, saying, "However, I'm certain he'll want to meet the Man who saved his son."

Eric smiled. "Your grace and charity are not exaggerated," he said formally, remembering the manners that had been drilled into him at his mother's insistence. Shela smiled a wide, perfect smile. Again, his heart swelled for her.

"I see you love Andaron horses," she said, noting his string. She turned her stallion to the east, her son and Nina with her, and kicked him into motion. The Lieutenant gave a whistle and called the 'Head out!' as Vulpe had before. The four of them led the Century to Hydrus.

"I've never had one before," Eric admitted. "I learned to ride on our own, shaggy ponies, because Myr is so close to the mountains."

"So how do they compare?" Shela asked him, and for an hour the two of them spoke about horses and riding and fighting, just as he might with any guest in his mother's house, now his. She asked to look at his sword, showed him the harpoon she kept slung across her back, and let him feel how smooth the shaft had been polished.

That harpoon! That new voice inside his head demanded of him. *Note it!* It felt at the same time too warm and too cold to his touch. Shela looked into his eyes the whole time as he regarded it, but said nothing.

As soon as they could see the great walls of Hydrus, Shela seemed to notice for the first time, "Nina, you're injured!"

"A scratch, my Lady," she said,

"Nonsense!" Shela informed her and reaching from her saddle, pushed the dressing aside. "Oh, Nina – this will leave a scar."

"It's fine," Nina assured her, and threw a glance at Eric.

Shela didn't miss that. "You did this?" she accused him.

Eric straightened. *'Out of favor so quickly?'* he wondered. "My apologies," he said, "and already to Nina, but it was, after all, a sword fight."

"He shattered my daggers and caught me off-guard." Nina admitted.

Without warning, the dressings fell away, slipping out from under her harness. Nina of the Aschire's skin stood alabaster and clean, even the thread from the stitches was gone.

"That's better," Shela informed them. Nina ran her left middle finger down her sternum, and Eric thought for a moment that she would cry.

"Mother," Vulpe sighed.

"No lady in my house will be scarred like a warrior," she informed him without looking. "I won't have it, and you're not your father, Chewee, and I'm not an Eldadorian Regular."

Vulpe shook his head. Nina simply remained quiet, looking at the city, saying nothing. They silently rode down out of the hills into the bazaar that had already opened outside of the city.

As Eric drew nearer, he saw that commerce had already restarted in Hydrus. A fleet of Eldadorian ships, and even some Confluni, clogged the wharves, with more anchored outside in the Bay, under the watchful eye of Eldadorian Sea Wolves.

The Emperor's design, a Sea Wolf's sails are cut square, not triangular like other ships of other countries, and they sport three and four masts, not one, each crowded with sails, full and white. Some sported brass funnels down their sides, meaning that they could launch 'Eldadorian Fire,' a liquid that burned in the air and on the water, so hot that nothing, not even sand, could extinguish it.

The people of Eldador, meaning the combined races from every nation on Fovea, crowded the bazaar. His own brother and sister Volkhydrans were selling their wares to these invaders as fast as they could carry them.

"You're surprised?" Vulpe asked him.

"They seem happy as Eldadorians," Eric said, simply, through gritted teeth. The city walls showed little damage, the gates already under repair. Hydrus had fallen with some kind of fight, however it couldn't have been much of one.

Eric could see an entire convoy of crates leaving the city for the wharves as they trotted closer. Nina, Shela and Vulpe saw this, too. "He has his books, then?" Vulpe asked his mother.

She nodded. "He loves the books," she said. "A treasure trove in this city, once we got into the vaults. Hundreds of them, and more art – all bound for Wisex now."

"What's Wisex?" Eric asked them. He'd never heard of that city or that nation before.

Shela straightened. "Wisex is the Emperor's personal city, at the meeting of the Safe and Mid Rivers," she said. "One day, it will be the heart of learning for all Eldadorian people, and all scholars will combine their knowledge in Wisex."

It sounded like a speech a politician would make, Eric thought, but he nodded. Normally, Fovean scholars from all nations were too busy hating each other to combine their knowledge anywhere to do anything.

"You must be tired from the road?" Nina asked him, and touched the back of his left hand with her right.

He nodded, realizing how far he'd ridden and how long it took. "I'll find a good inn in the city," he said.

"Nonsense!" Shela informed him. "You saved my son's life, Sir Eric. You're a guest of the Emperor of Eldador and a Hero of the Empire, and you'll eat and sleep in the palace."

The palace where Duke Dragor's blood had likely stained the carpets, Eric thought. He was beholden to Dragor, as Count Tezzen's vassal.

"I'm honored, my Lady," he said, and lowered his head again. If they could take Dragor with a city full of warriors, Eric on three horses wouldn't be much effort for them.

"Nina, could you see to him?" Shela asked off-handedly. "I'm going to spend some time with my son, before he tries to kill himself again."

"Mother," Vulpe complained.

"He *is* like his father," Nina agreed, grinning.

Eric opened his mouth, then closed it. For a moment, he thought she meant *him*.

She stood up in her saddle, and said, "This way," to Eric, turning her horse by its reins. He followed her, away from the main crowd and the Century, around the bazaar and, after almost two daheeri, to a side-entrance into the city.

"This is new, as far as we can tell," she informed him, as Wolf Soldier guards nodded to her and opened a side gate. "In Galnesh Eldador, there is a direct entrance to the royal stables, and we think that Dragor admired it and wanted one for himself."

"What happened to Dragor?" Eric asked her, as they guided their horses inside to an enclosed stable.

She looked sideways at him from her saddle. "We beat him," she answered.

"But to him, personally," Eric pressed her.

She shrugged. "Dungeons, I suppose," she said. "I didn't hear about any great sword fight between him and the Emperor, neither did I hear about him surrendering. The city fell fighting to the last warrior – normally the royals are the last to die."

Eric nodded, but in his heart, his blood boiled. These were *Volkhydrans*, by Law! These were his kinsmen, whom she so easily dismissed. There were stories of how Lupus shamed and tortured those who opposed him – his own father, now, he realized. Law taught that the sins of the father, if unrepented, could fall to the son.

Eric thought that he might have a lot of penance, among other things in his future.

Chapter Eight:

A Volkhydran Man

They put their horses up in a private stable reserved for the palace. There weren't many horses there, although at the same time, Eric doubted that there could be room here for the thousands that the Emperor was said to have brought. There must be either another pasture somewhere, or they were free-standing the Emperor's herds with handlers outside the city.

He could believe either.

Nina took him by the forearm out of the stables and through a back entrance to the palace, climbing a winding stair up the hill that it stood on. Eric had never been here before, and was surprised to see the evidence of wear all over the palace. Corners had long since worn off of ancient stones, floors showed paths down the center and discolorations in the spaces more difficult to clean. The workers from Eldador had already begun work scrubbing and patching, restoring ancient stairways and bridges. Dwarves supervised here and there among the Men and Uman as they restored what looked to be flying bridges.

"He doesn't waste any time, does he?" Eric asked Nina as they climbed to another guarded door, two Wolf Soldiers with pikes on either side of it.

"I wish he'd waste a little," Nina said. "We all worry that he drives himself too hard. No sooner did he plant his flag here, then he headed north to seek out Gharf Bendenson, your Volkhydran King."

"So he *does* plan to roll up the Llorando?" Eric pressed her.

"Not so far as I know," Nina said. She nodded to the Wolf Soldier, who made a fist over his heart for her and opened the door. They both fixed her with their eyes, as if they expected her to strike them without warning. Eric felt as if they barely noticed him at all.

They entered a passage made all of stone, with light coming from shafts in its ceiling. Eric marveled at that – how could anyone build a palace with holes all cut in it? He pointed it out to Nina.

"It's done with mirrors," Nina informed him. "They have a central shaft down the center of the palace, with other things called 'ducts,' all pointed to the sky. This widens out to highly polished cones lined with steel mirrors. If you keep the mirrors clean, then the light from the sun as it moves through the sky hits one and then the other, and then the light from the sky, as well as air, is moved through the palace to all of these places, and while the sun is in the sky, you've got light in all of these places and never have to light a torch."

"You know how to do this?" Eric asked her, as they moved down the passage. The place was quiet as a rabbit's den, although here and there he saw the bloodstains that marked the fight that had happened here. The palace had indeed not gone without a fight.

Nina shook her head. "The Emperor figured it out," she said. "He has a mind for these things. We've actually had a Scitai – Karel of Stone – drop down into the ducts and verify him."

Eric had never met a Scitai – of a race of people who almost never grew taller than three feet, and who lived on the Silent Isle with the Uman-Chi. They were expert archers and lived among the trees like the Aschire supposedly did.

They turned at the end of the passage and came to a winding stair. Climbing this, they passed more Wolf Soldier guards at different doors and then came to a landing, where they could move either up the same stairs, or cross a wide, empty room, with circular walls as one might find in a tower, to a side stairs. Nina crossed to that.

The room had wide windows to either side. Eric looked out through them and saw the city from the inside, with people crawling like ants over the streets and byways of Hydrus.

He couldn't help himself – he stepped up to the window, just an opening carved in the wall, and looked outside, placing his hands on the warm, stone edging. In that new part of his mind, he told himself that he should be using this opportunity to plan the re-invasion of the city, but he couldn't help his own wonder.

"So many people," he said to Nina, who stepped up next to him.

"I forget the effect that this can have," she said. "When I came to Galnesh Eldador, I stood on a wall and looked down into a crowd of thousands, as Duke Rancor Mordetur was made a king. Before then, I had never seen fifty living beings at the same time, and I wondered how they could stand it – how they could live together, packed like ants in a hill."

"The whole city of Myr wouldn't fill the inner palace," he said, without thinking.

She laid her hand on the middle of his back. "Time enough for gazing," she said. "The Emperor could return at any time, and you'll want to be refreshed when you meet him."

He nodded. She led him up the side stairway to darker rooms, unlit or with empty wall sconces, the stonework looking newer and not meeting evenly with the outer walls, as he'd seen.

"This is new, isn't it?" Eric asked Nina. She nodded.

"Dragor's father, we think, must have built side rooms here for his warriors," she said. She pulled a door open and entered a room with a cot and a chest of drawers. She crossed that and opened a door on the other side, where they found a larger room with a window and a bath tub, a brazier burning in one corner under a steel drum. She crossed to the brazier and opened a steel box next to it, pulled out a shovel full of coal and dumped it into the brazier.

"This heats the water in the drum," she said. She knocked on the drum and it didn't ring. "Good," she added, "it's been kept full. It takes a few minutes, but the water is piped through the brazier, as it cools, and rises back up to the drum as it heats. When the vents on top start to steam, you have hot water, and you can dump it to the tub."

"That's very clever," Eric said, nodding.

She shook her head. "Not really," she sighed. "It can get too hot and scald you, or it can boil away and crack the pipes. If you put too much coal, or not enough, the whole thing doesn't work."

"Oh," Eric said. He found it disappointing, actually – he didn't think he was clever enough to design it.

She turned to him and took his furs in her hands. "However," she said, "it's better than carrying buckets, and it fills from rainwater on the top of the tower, so if you watch it, it isn't bad."

Eric nodded, then pulled his head back as she started to unlace his furs.

"What – what are you doing?" he asked her.

"You need a bath," she informed him.

"I had a bath in Myr," he informed her. He ran a hand through his hair and showed it to her. "See? No lice."

She shook her head and pulled his furs open, revealing his chest. She tried to push them off of his shoulders, but he stepped back.

"You're going to bathe me?" he asked her.

"I owe you for stitching me," she said, stepping back up to him. She took a firmer grip on his furs this time – he couldn't think how he could politely step away.

"But – but Shela," he spluttered.

She pushed his furs down his arm, pinning them at his sides. She took his shaggy leather pants' waist in her two hands starting pulling at his lacing.

"Hey!" That dark side of his mind was just chuckling at him now.

"What?" she asked him. "Shy? Never been bathed by a woman?"

"Well, my mother," he said, shrugging out of his furs. Behind him, his sword clattered to the ground. He looked behind him, fearing for the blade, and Nina pulled his lacings open in a single move.

"Ho!" he protested, taking Nina by her wrists with his hands. Her skin was warm to his touch, the look in her eyes was one of some happy predator, laughing at him as she readied herself for her kill.

"Nina, this is *not*, I mean," he spluttered, then lowered his head and sighed.

"You'll *see* me," he admitted, finally.

"Well," she said, "you've seen me."

"I had to," he said. "I mean, well, you're very beautiful – but I had to stitch you."

She smiled. "I'm beautiful?" she asked him.

More of that chuckling in the back of his mind. He'd had girls flirt with him before, but Law's children did *not* behave this way, and this was sacred to a married couple. Certainly, a man's wife would have to see him naked – but he barely knew Nina.

"What if someone comes in and finds us?" he retreated, finally.

She chuckled and stepped back from him, leaving his pants hanging low on his hips. She reached behind her neck and she released the top of her halter, then as it dropped to her waist, she untied the back, letting the piece of black leather fall to the floor.

As he watched her, she unfastened the lacings of her own leather pants, then dropped them, revealing herself before him in a cotton cloth twisted on her loins.

She cast that to one side.

"Now you have to remove your pants, or you'll dishonor me," she informed him. "Would you shame a woman, Eric of Myr?"

He never would, he knew. He'd never done anything like this before, never had to deal with this. Nina was older than he and more experienced, clearly – he feared no other warrior, would draw his sword on a man twice his age or more, but this woman left him defenseless.

Behind her, the top vents from the drum began to steam. As his pants hit the floor and he stepped out of them, revealed to Nina of the Aschire, he felt as if he could sympathize with them.

***

She turned a few valves and water flooded steaming into the bath tub. He was about to step into it, but she made him go relieve himself first. When he returned from the bucket in the other room, he found her waiting in the water with a brush and a cake of soap.

"Oh," he said. "Do you want me to come back?"

She shook her head. "I'm going to guess that mother was the only other woman who's seen you naked?"

"I think I already said that," he said, and stepped into the tub. He immediately slipped on the slick interior and fell backwards into it. The splash soaked them both. She laughed and moved up next to him.

The warm water soaked into his tired muscles. He realized all of a sudden that he was being ridiculous – his mother's maids had washed him as a child and he'd thought nothing of it. Nina was a servant of the House Mordetur and was doing what the Empress had told her.

She turned him around and scrubbed his hair. She used her brush and soap to scrub him from his shoulders to his toes, giving him a thrill as she handled him, grinning all the while.

When she'd scrubbed between his toes, she handed him the soap and brush and said, "Have you washed a girl before?"

His eyebrows rose. "No, never," he admitted.

"Well," she said, "I'm not a horse, so be gentle with me. The dirt comes off without much scrubbing."

He scrubbed her hair as she had his. It grew out luxurious and thick and reminded him of his mother's. He washed her back and shoulders with the brush, her front with a wash cloth. He found himself looking for some remnant of the scar he'd seen and found none.

"You like my breasts, it seems," she informed him, hunter's gleam back full force.

"I've never, I mean – um, I was looking for the scar," he admitted.

She saddened a little. "Yes," she said. "Shela does that – I actually meant to keep that scar as a reminder."

"To keep your guard?" he asked her. He looked up into her eyes and saw a different look, not hurt so much as disappointment.

"No," she informed him.

"How far, I mean, what more do you want me to –" he asked her.

She had her grin back. She turned and pressed her back into his chest. "I did all of you," she informed him.

He used the cloth for the rest of her. He couldn't help letting his fingers drift. He'd never seen the parts of a woman and, as much as he expected her to protest him, he got nothing more than contented little sighs from her. He finished with her toes as she had, her facing him with one foot in his lap and the other in his hand. The soap clouded the water, which by then had gone cold.

"Are we done?" Eric asked her.

She turned and lay on him, her breasts on his stomach, her wet purple hair framing her eyes. He noted that her upturned eyebrows gave her face a sort of surprised look – he'd been thinking that he had that effect on her, but it seemed to him then that it was just her face.

Different species could be strange, he knew.

"Unless there's something else you can think of doing," she informed him.

In the cold tub, there really wasn't anything. He took the edges of the tub in either hand, and she swished back from him. Being more careful this time, he stood, the water running off from him.

To his horror, she reached for him, not some passing brush stroke, but actually took his manhood in her hand. His body reacted as if in no consideration for his mind, a rush flowing up from his toes to the back of his head, as if he'd taken all of the warmth from the bathwater into himself and then released it right then.

"Nina!" he gasped, trying to back away from her. Unfortunately, what he found instead was the edge of the tub behind him, and his heels its slick surface.

He crashed over the edge, the back of his head slamming into the hard stone floor. The world exploded in a flash around him, and then there was nothing.

***

He awoke naked in a warm bed, an Uman in a white robe staring into his face.

He recognized a priest of Adriam. Uman were a long-lived people, their lives crossing as many as twenty decades, though rarely. They were more gifted magically than the race of Men, however it was Men who had the truly great Wizards and Sorceresses.

He noted the brown eyes, the silver hair, the pointed ears, lobeless and small on the side of the Uman's head. The symbol of Adriam, the All-Father, hung on a gold pendant around his neck.

Eric worshipped the god Law – his symbol the closed fist. Adriam's was an open hand, the giving god. His priests were healers.

Out of his vision, he heard two women's voices – one he knew instantly was Nina's, the other he recognized as Shela Mordetur.

"What could you have been thinking?" she demanded.

"He's, he's just so –" Nina sputtered.

"Yes, he's very so," Shela informed her. "He's barely in his teens, Nina – you have no business with him."

"You weren't there, Shela," Nina protested. "He – the way he moved, the way he fought -"

"Nina, I will *not* have this," Shela cut her off. "You may have paralyzed him – you took your pleasure with a child -"

"The sword makes him a man," Nina interrupted. "Among my own people -"

"You aren't among your own people," Shela warned, her voice dropping an octave, "But I can fix that!"

"Shela!"

"He's awake," Eric heard Vulpe's voice. "Perhaps our priest can tell us his condition?"

"Your name?" the priest asked him.

"Eric of Myr," he said. Beyond him, he saw Nina's face, then she was pulled away and he saw the Empress. She might have been an Empress, but right then she was the mother of the Empire, and she oversaw a broken child.

"Raise your right hand to my shoulder, Eric," the priest told him.

He did it. His hand felt a little strange, but he gripped the Uman's shoulder.

"Very good, Eric," he said. "Now, wiggle your feet for me."

He did so, leaving his hand on the Uman's shoulder.

"Again," the Uman ordered him. He did so.

He heard a sigh from somewhere.

The Uman straightened. "The damage is repaired," the Uman informed the rest of them. "He'll walk, he'll fight, he'll still be strong. Let him rest for a day – alone."

"Who'll tend –" he heard Nina's voice, then the crack of a slap.

"Your quarters," he heard Shela say. "Stay there – I'll speak with the Emperor and decide if we have any room for you here anymore."

Eric heard a door open and close. The priest murmured something to the others in the room. Eric just closed his eyes, exhausted.

He could remember being in the tub with Nina, and then her scaring him and him falling.

"He's sleeping," he heard Vulpe say.

"Did you know about this?" Shela asked him.

"Well," Vulpe said, "after they fought, I sent him to her to make his peace. She let him stitch her, so I knew they had something going on."

"You should have told me right away," Shela admonished him.

"If I'd known they'd split meat, I would have," Vulpe said. "But –"

He said more, but Eric was drifting off and didn't hear it. In his mind, he could see Nina with the piece of hard tack in her teeth, in the darkness of her tent.

Supposedly that meant something.

He was roused a little later – he couldn't tell how long – when someone knocked on the door and said, "Empress?"

"What?"

"My lady," the voice was strange – he didn't recognize it. "Couriers are returned from the capitol, Lady. Grave news."

"Well, we can never have enough of that," Shela spat. "What is it?"

"Shall we go in private, Lady?" the voice asked.

He heard a sigh. "I've had a very bad week, Almerk," Shela informed the messenger. "I've got one child trying to kill himself, one trying to mate, a stranger saving one to mate the other, and now your bad news. Just tell it to me, while I still have my patience."

"Majesty…" the messenger pleaded.

"*Now*, Almerck."

For a moment, nothing, then a sigh, and the messenger, Almerck, said, "My Lady, from the hand of Duke Tartan Stowe, of Angador, now sitting regent in the capitol, 'We regret to inform you that the Uman-Chi have attacked the capitol through your Central Communications portal and, as a result of the attack, both Central Communications, Duke Hectar Gelgelden, his son Hectaro and your daughter, Princess Lee, are lost."

Chapter Nine:

A Mourning After

Eric woke with the sun, as he had for most of his life. An Uman woman attended him – smiling at him as he opened up his eyes. As if she'd read his mind, she pointed to a bucket in the corner and she left the room.

He couldn't believe how much he'd held in. He must have soaked in half that tub. The previous day's actions kept flashing back on him – what he'd seen, what he'd touched, what he'd done.

He'd just finished when Vulpe entered through the one door. He took two steps into the room, made a face and looked at the bucket. "We're going for a walk," he informed Eric. "I was going to ask if you were strong enough, but if you're not, I'm not either."

Eric shook his head and picked up his furs, slipping easily into them and his boots. He checked his sword, belted it over his shoulder, and followed Vulpe out the door and down the tower steps. He was still sleeping in the cluster of rooms that Nina had brought him to, but he didn't see her.

"Your mother seemed upset," Eric informed him as they descended the stairs.

"You remember that?"

"Hard not to."

Vulpe chuckled. They found the bottom landing, where a Wolf Soldier squad waited. They formed up after the two young men and followed them to the stables. Eric kept his own council – he didn't completely trust the Wolf Soldiers, much as Vulpe seemed to ignore them.

"What are your thoughts with Nina?" Vulpe asked him, as they neared the entrance to the stables.

Eric almost tripped. "Well," he said, "I kind of hope she doesn't try to kill me again."

"She does that a lot," Vulpe noted. "But then she lets you heal her."

"That she does," Eric agreed. "Are we riding?"

"If there are any horses left," Vulpe said as they entered the forward paddocks. "Father left West with every warrior he could mount."

"What?" Eric was stunned – how could he have come and gone so fast?

"While you were sleeping," Vulpe said. "Which is a shame, because he wanted to meet you. He did look in, but the priest said you should be allowed to rest until you roused yourself."

"He couldn't wait a day?"

"He *did* wait a day," Vulpe answered him, walking past the empty paddocks. "How long do you think you were asleep?"

"Overnight?" Eric somehow believed that that wasn't true now.

"Try a day, two more nights and then part of today," Vulpe informed him. "I probably caught Nina in there ten times, and mother two more."

"She felt bad?"

Vulpe looked sideways at him shook his head. "Could you tell me something, and be honest?" he asked.

They'd finally come to Eric's horses. As Vulpe had warned, they were the only ones left. He pulled his saddle from where someone had hung it and indicated that Vulpe could have his pick of the horses. "Always," he said.

"Did you really share meat with her?"

"You sent me into her tent with it," Eric answered him.

Vulpe scowled. "No, did she, for example, take a piece of meat in her mouth, and ask you to take the other end of it –"

Eric nodded. "Oh, yes – never done that before."

Vulpe chuckled. "I should hope not."

Eric looked sideways at him. He was getting grouchy. He'd have to wait longer now to see the Emperor, Nina wasn't around and he wanted her, and now Vulpe was making some weird joke.

"You have no idea?" Vulpe challenged him.

"What?" he demanded, and threw down the saddle. The Wolf Soldier guards started. "What is it, Chewee? Yes, we shared meat – no, I've never done it before. Yes, we took a bath together. Yes, I fell out of it and smacked my head, what else?"

Vulpe took him by the upper arm. "Peace, Eric," he said. "It comes as a surprise to all of us, that's all. All my life, Nina's been like an older sister, almost like another mother to me. I never really thought of her with someone else, but I suppose she's always been a woman, too."

Eric wasn't getting this. He squatted down to pick up his saddle.

"Among Aschire," Vulpe said, "the courting is done mostly by the women. One of the things they do is to cut a piece of meat, take it in their teeth and offer it to a man they want."

"Oh," Eric said, then thought about it. "Oh," he said again, and dropped the saddle.

"Oh, really?" he demanded. Vulpe had a grin on his face a daheer wide.

"You're going to ruin that saddle," Vulpe warned him.

"Where – where is she, I mean –"

"Not to worry," Vulpe said, picking up the saddle. He took a long step and tossed it up onto the top rail of the paddock fence. "She went with father, she'll be back in a few days. Mother is convinced that she's spent too much time with women and children, and some fighting will have her back to her old self."

"You don't seem so sure," Eric said, as Vulpe reached for his own saddle and threw it up next to Eric's.

"I haven't known Nina as long as Lee and my parents have," he said, "but I've spent a lot of time with her since she started to notice males. I also know that when Nina of the Aschire decides that she wants something, she gets it, and if someone tries to take it away, it only makes her want it more."

"Then what should I do?" Eric asked him. He didn't like this – being some *thing* that a woman wanted, getting advice on how to handle it from a twelve-year-old.

Vulpe climbed up the fence next to him and dropped down on the other side of the paddock. "I don't know, my friend," he said. "Imagine your face on purple-haired children?"

***

They rode for hours. Vulpe apparently appreciated good Andaron horses, and Eric just needed to blow off some steam. Young girls had flirted with him more obviously in recent years, but never a woman, and never with Nina's ferocity.

He couldn't help feeling stupid for not seeing it.

They returned to the stable to find Shela there, pacing the paddocks, dressed out in her leathers as she had been when Eric had first seen them.

"Where have you been?" she demanded.

"You said to take him riding," Vulpe informed her from the saddle.

She gritted her teeth. "I didn't mean to spend the day," she informed him. "We're a family in mourning, Chewee – you could spend some time with your mother."

That rang a bell for Eric. He remembered, just as he was drifting off – something about a Duke, and his son, and something called Central Communications and –

A princess!

"Oh, your Majesty," he exclaimed. "Oh, my Lady, I am so sorry."

She tried to smile, but her red rimmed eyes betrayed her. She'd been informed that her daughter had been lost in some sort of invasion of the capital.

His half-sister – a sibling he'd never meet.

He'd always wanted a sister.

"Is that where the Emperor has gone?" Eric asked. Vulpe shook his head.

"He spent a while raging," the boy said. "Swore he'd see the flesh that lay behind the Uman-Chi king's eyes – that sort of thing. Then we were informed yesterday that Gharf Bendenson had raided our supply train from Medya."

"Woe to him," Shela said. "Yonega Waya, my husband, rode out of here with his mounted warriors – I think that Gharf has seen his last day as a Fovean by now."

Eric's heart constricted. He had a responsibility to his King to fight these invaders.

He calmed himself. He couldn't do that now. The deeper he got in with the family, the more useful he could be later.

"And you, my lady," Eric asked. "What of you."

She sighed. "I miss my little girl," she said, and now she couldn't keep the tears off of her face. "I thought myself so lucky – three strong children and all living. I thought that this was the Emperor's luck, worn off on me."

He reached down to her, and she took his hand. He looked into her beautiful, brown eyes. Yes, this was the woman who had taken his father away from his mother's side. But here was a woman who'd lost a child, and as a fellow member of the race of Men, he felt in his heart that he had to console her.

"Your son informs me that you like to ride," he said finally. She tried to smile up at him.

"I think not today, Sir Eric," she said, "but I do appreciate your kind gesture."

"As I told you, Eric," Vulpe said, catching on. "That's an Andaron stallion that you have there, and mother isn't a young woman any more."

"What?" she protested. That got her.

"Well, mother," Vulpe said. "You're a woman with *three* births behind her."

She snorted and, without using her hands, leapt up the side of the paddock, put her foot on the top rail and leapt onto the stallion's back. The horse snorted and crow-hopped, she took it's mane in her fist and turned him with her hips and legs.

She backed him as deep into the paddock as she could, then shouted, "Hya!" and kicked him in the ribs. The stallion launched itself at the paddock walls, faster and faster, then leapt for the rail, its front hooves scuffing the wood.

Shela rose up off of the stallion's bare back, then seated herself soundly on his withers as he landed. The stallion took off for the stable entrance, the two other horses leaping after it, as the three took off into the afternoon.

The ride took Eric's breath away. He heard Vulpe laugh. The two of them grieved as Andarons, riding hard, the wind in their hair.

He hadn't really grieved for his own mother. She'd left him. He'd had a mission. Aileen lay deep in Earth's bosom now, at peace without her Rancor.

For a little while Eric let the tears flow, where he could excuse them in the wind, for the mother he'd lost and the half-sister that he'd never know.

Chapter Ten:

We are not Invaders

For five days, rumors ranged in and out of Volkhydro from the plains. Lupus had engaged Gharf Bendenson's troops and taken back his supplies. Lupus had crushed a troop of Volkhydrans who tried to stand against him. When they tried to draw him into an ambush, Lupus saw it at the last minute and crushed it.

Shela haunted the city like a ghost – her eyes telling the world of her grief for her daughter. She didn't rage. She didn't crush her enemies as the Emperor did. She enveloped grief as one would a child, Eric noted, and held it close to her bosom.

Eric really wanted to hate her and feel as if she'd gotten what she deserved. These people had come to his nation to conquer it. They'd killed warriors by the tens of thousands. A marching army of mothers felt just the way that Shela did, or worse, for the invaders who had come to their nation and killed their sons and daughters.

Along with the violence, of course, went the atrocities. The atrocities were unavoidable. Warriors who'd just risked everything and come out alive usually wanted to celebrate their conquests. They wanted to crush their enemies. They wanted to dominate.

Volkhydran women had made themselves a little camp outside of the city – there were more than one hundred of them, shunned by their families, the raped victims of Eldadorian soldiers. Their plight spoke to Eric. On the fifth day, Eric had ridden out to them with Vulpe and his third horse, loaded to its knees' bending with the weight of the goods it was carrying. Eric knew better than to just ride down there with the goods – there'd be a riot. He needed to get them to a smaller portion of the women, who could be trusted to distribute them to the rest.

"You shouldn't let your warriors rape," Eric admonished Vulpe. The boy sat the other Andaron horse in black doublet and hose. He and his mother had stuck to black clothes this week.

"Try and stop them," he said. "You have Volkhydrans in your armies here. They all think the same way, they all act the same way. I have every race and some of them hate each other. Confluni will rape a Volkhydran woman just to show her how much they hate Volkhydrans."

Eric shook his head. His mother wasn't raped, but she was taken advantage of by a foreign warrior and he'd left her with a child. He didn't like that – he didn't like how these poor daughters would be shunned by their families, some just until their next cycle, some forever while they raised their bastards.

All so that foreign warriors could exult in their victory and express their politics.

He couldn't stand it.

"There," he said, of a group of women off to one said. "That will do."

"Ride down there and they'll run," Vulpe told him. "They've been reinvaded a few times, I'm told, even by Volkhydrans. They're marred women – no one is fighting for them."

And that was it, of course. No sooner did Vulpe mention it than, on the other side of the small camp, a troop of warriors emerged from the road between two hills, their intent clear. The women began shouting to each other, some gathering up their possessions, some hiking up their skirts and running already.

"Those are Eldadorians," Vulpe warned him as he pulled his sword. That new and more aggressive part of his brain was already egging him on.

"Not for long," he informed Vulpe, and kicked his horse into a trot.

Eric had fought before. He'd fought against greater numbers as a part of his training. He'd fought on horseback and he'd fought on foot.

He knew he wasn't any exceptional warrior – he'd lost more fights in practice than he'd won – but Tezzen had always told him, always drilled into his students, that the battle didn't always go to the better trained warrior. It often went to the one that wanted it more.

When Eric saw the leers, heard the screams, marked the Eldadorians in armor and with their swords, running a dozen strong into these Volkhydran daughters in their weakness, he knew that, no matter what else, he wanted it more.

His world turned red, and he kicked his horse into a canter. That angry part of his brain had been calling for some sort of action. This time Eric let it have its say.

The women screamed, then screamed again when they thought themselves surrounded. They parted like a wave before him and his one horse, running from a dozen Eldadorian Regulars on horseback, three of these already off their mounts and pulling women to the ground.

The ones in front looked up from their victims to see a mounted Volkhydran swinging a sword and closing fast. Eldadorian training took over – the remaining nine dropped into three ranks of three, their swords all out on the right, ready to meet him.

At the last moment, Eric pulled his mount to his right, passing the warriors on their left. Switching hands, he cleaved at them with his black blade, two of the warriors raising their armored sleeves as shields.

It didn't help them – two arms and a head fell to the ground, Eric barely slowing. Tezzen had insisted that his students learn to fight left handed, now Eric knew why. He wheeled the spirited Andaron mount on a short turn and then drove his heels into its ribs, racing for his enemies.

Six horses trying to move as a unit, mixing with three whose riders were either dead or in shock, couldn't turn as fast. Eric cut behind the confused mounts, hitting a one-armed man across the lower back and two more across the shoulders. The dark part of his brain exulted, advising him, instructing him, giving him strategy. He cut the mount to the left and then spun it to the right, the enemy horses crashing into each other and the mounts with dead riders trying to herd with the others. One reared, its dead rider falling out behind him, hanging by an ankle to the stirrup. The spooked horse brained one of the still-living riders with a huge hoof, then landed on all fours and kicked out at the body it dragged, catching another horse in the ribs and its rider in the leg. Eric heard the bone snap.

Six were down and three ran for the hills, back the way they'd come. The warriors who'd been on the ground were already running for their mounts – no one had even come close to laying a hand on Eric.

Now he saw Vulpe riding past him to the other Eldadorians. One turned with his sword out, then recognized Vulpe Mordetur. He slammed the sword into its sheath and made a fist over his heart. The two others saw him and followed suit.

Vulpe pulled his mount up short, staring down imperiously on the three warriors. They dropped their hands as one and stood at attention, waiting for his orders.

"What have you men to say for yourselves?" Vulpe demanded of them.

To their credit, they didn't break. One stepped forward, and said, "No excuse, Lord Commander."

"I want those other soldiers," he ordered them. "Present yourselves in front of the barracks. I'll get there when I'm done here."

They saluted as one, and turned for their horses. Vulpe let them mount up and watched them ride away.

Eric trotted his mount up to Vulpe's side. Already, the women were coming back, shy as sheep, waiting for these saviors to treat them like the last warriors had.

"What happens to them?" Eric asked Vulpe, as soon as they were out of earshot.

"There's six," he said. "I'll pick one at random and order the others to hang him."

"They'll do that?"

Vulpe looked up at him from horseback. "They will," he said. "They know their crime, they know their fate.

"You think we're monsters, we're invaders, but we're not," he said. "I see the look on your face sometimes, the anger. Don't be ashamed that you're proud of your country, Eric. I'm proud of mine, and I don't blame you when you're angry at us."

"You come here as invaders," Eric snarled through clenched teeth.

"We do," Vulpe agreed. "But my father will unite these Fovean nations under one banner. He'll end the wars that kill us by the thousands every year."

"By killing us by the thousands now," Eric said.

Vulpe smiled a half-smile. "I don't think it will all be as bad as here," he said. "This was engineered by the Uman-Chi. They called for this battle."

Eric didn't like it, but he wasn't going to argue with his half-brother. He needed the boy's good graces to get to the father. The two letters in their scroll case still rested inside of his furs, against his skin.

Together, they handed out the bread and goods to the wary women, giving them, if nothing else, some respite against their hunger and their ill luck. Eric wondered which of them would be grateful of the Emperor's efforts to liberate them.

As they returned to Hydrus, Eric noted that the city flew the pennons of the Emperor himself, the Wolf's head banner. Any member of the royal family could fly them, but only the Emperor himself had the banner with red eyes. To the western side, the city's stable gates were open and Volkhydrans and Uman servants were scrambling to contain a huge herd of horses.

Vulpe laughed and kicked his mount. Eric trailed him, pulling the pack horse as well. This could be it, he thought. The Emperor might well be in the stable where they were headed, or waiting to greet his son and the man who'd saved him.

Finally, Eric thought, there would be a little justice in a Volkhydro that wanted for it.

Chapter Eleven:

A Cruel God

They entered the side gate to the Ducal stables – they stepped past Eldadorian Regulars and Wolf Soldiers, warriors who'd seen tough fighting and bore the marks of it with bloody bandages and dented armor. To one side, a man grimaced as two others set his broken arm. To the other, three were putting a mare down – her flank too badly scored ever to save her.

In a stall whose ceiling had been elevated and whose sides had been reinforced, a huge white stallion stood with his neck arched, a warrior in corrugated armor brushing down the wet print from his saddle and his cinch.

The Emperor of Eldador, Rancor Mordetur, called Lupus, the Conqueror.

Eric's father.

He kicked his horse, but Vulpe put a hand on his forearm.

"You won't get within twenty feet of him," Vulpe warned.

"What?"

"Look, there and there," the boy said, pointing to foot soldiers, standing with their arms behind them, in the gray tabards of Wolf Soldiers.

"They'd kill you just because they don't know you," he said. "And with Lee gone – they'd make it bloody just to prove a point. The Imperial Family has been threatened, Eric. They'll kill without thinking."

"Can you?" Eric asked him, and Vulpe smiled.

"I'm going to put up this horse, because the horse doesn't care who my father is," he said. "That's how an Andaron thinks. Then I'm going to go to my father, and tell him that you'd like to meet him. He'll come to you after that."

"You're sure?"

"As sure as I can be," Vulpe said. "These aren't good times, Eric. Lee was my father's joy. He might not be in a speaking mood, and if he isn't, then he won't see you.

"You're dealing with a man with a lot of weight hanging from him. You might consider yourself light as a pebble, but a pebble can cripple a horse."

Eric nodded. They brought their horses to the paddocks that Eric had been given, and they brushed the animals down. Eric did their hooves as Vulpe departed to find his father.

Eric waited a long time, but he didn't have a lot of sense of it. On one hand, he felt every second, and on the other, the minutes flew by with agonizing speed. The sun had started to set. He'd curried out his horses' tails until they shone before Vulpe returned.

The boy was disturbed. He'd been saddled with a lot, this Vulpe – if rumor had it right, he'd led the Eldadorian Millennia into combat on three occasions, and been victorious. To kill so many would weigh on the soul of one so young.

Already, Eric was seeing the eyes of the Eldadorians that he'd just run through, and he'd considered that a just cause.

"Your Highness," Eric greeted him formally.

Vulpe grinned his half-grin. "For love of War, call me Chewee today," he said. "Vulpe Mordetur has a lot to bear."

"Chewee, then," Eric said. "I take it that the Emperor isn't in the mood to meet many people."

Chewee shook his head, his smile disappearing. "He had a lot to say to me," he said. "My father – his thoughts run so deep, a man should drown in all of that."

"Perhaps the cost of this war has come home to him?" Eric suggested.

Chewee nodded. "I think you're right. He'll sue for peace tomorrow. He plans to send the Druid, Dilvesh of the Daff Kanaar, to the Fovean High Council in his name."

"What?" Eric couldn't believe it. Had the loss struck him so hard? Had he felt the death of his own child so deeply? If so, wouldn't he now welcome another one?

Chewee nodded. "The Emperor will remain here, and with his warriors safeguard these Volkhydrans who've sided with him. He'll brook no retaliation against the people who supported him."

Eric nodded – wise decision. Gharf Bendenson would skin them all alive as a lesson to the rest.

"As for me, I'm to leave here, Eric. I'm to return home – not mine, but to my people's home. To Andoron."

Eric felt his brow furrow. That made no sense – there'd be no security for Vulpe alone in Andoron, and plenty who'd take that opportunity to rob the Emperor of another child.

"I'd like to bring you with me," Chewee said. "You've been a good friend, Eric, and you're hell with that sword. Every member of my family has trusted body guards – I'd have you be mine."

"I'm honored," Eric informed him. "But I've other business, Chewee. You know – I'm bound to see the Emperor on behalf of my Count –"

"Your Count is dead," Vulpe replied. "Tezzen raided the grain wagons – father crushed him on the plains, and a good part of Bendenson's army with him. What's left is scattered – there will be no Volkhydran resistance. There'll be no negotiation."

Eric felt the pommel of his sword in his palm before he realized it. This new, angry portion of brain railed. How *dare* he? How dare he remark so casually that his father - *their* father - had just dispatched his kinsmen and his family?

The blood price for this would drown one hundred warriors.

"Be angry, Eric," Vulpe informed him. He reached out and took his half-brother by the forearm. "We'll need angry men where we're going."

"To Andoron?" Eric spat, shaking free from the younger boy. "I don't know anything about Andoron. I can't protect you there."

"You can," Chewee ensured him, "with the help of fifty thousand of my father's Regulars. While the Emperor sues for peace, we'll be taking the city of Chatoos."

***

From the stables they walked to the barracks. At the barracks stood six warriors in full Eldadorian green, their breastplates and their boots polished.

One of them was going to look good as he swung.

Vulpe shook his head – Eric had forgotten about them, and he felt sure that the young Prince had as well.

He marched himself right up to the one at the center of them. "Sergeant?" he demanded.

"No excuses, Sir," the Uman said. "We did a stupid thing, unworthy of the Regulars. We know the penalty."

Eric nodded. He inhaled, closed his eyes. He'd pick one at random, Eric knew, and then the others would hang him.

They'd have been taught some sort of lesson – the ones that didn't swing.

"Liar," Eric heard himself say.

Vulpe opened his eyes, regarded Eric.

"No excuses," Eric parroted him. "No reason – we just got it into our head one day, 'Let's rape!' No, Lord Commander, that's a lie."

The sergeant regarded him but didn't say anything. Even hating them, Eric had to admire the discipline.

"What are you saying, Eric?" Vulpe asked him.

"You plan to kill one – they'll do it again. The ones who don't die will laugh about it. One will swing and, before the night is over, one of them will be back to that camp.

"No, Vulpe, that's not the way to show them. I have a better way."

***

Eric sat his tired mount, Vulpe next to him, overlooking the camp of disgraced women. They'd tried to marshal out their food and bedding, but already most of it was gone. Too much wealth, he knew, was just a dare to others passing by to rob them.

Down into the camp, six naked warriors marched single file. The woman hadn't noticed them yet, but they would.

"You're cruel, Viscount Eric of Myr," Vulpe told him.

"Heartless as a snowstorm."

Eric could accept that.

One of the women screamed, seeing them. Others took up the shout. They started to run, but then they saw the men were alone, and unarmed. Defenseless. Were these other victims? Were these desperate seekers, much like they?

But then they were recognized. Women looked to the hills and saw Vulpe and Eric, and *they* were recognized. Then the reality of the situation dawned on these women.

These raped, battered, shamed and abused women.

Their scream was a terrible thing to hear as, more like a wolf pack than a group of women, they swarmed the defenseless men, outnumbered more than ten to one.

Eric turned his mount around. Vulpe followed him.

"You're a cold and vicious man, Sir Eric," Vulpe repeated.

Eric wondered what his mother would have done, if she could have gotten some justice like that.

He felt he'd live a better life, never knowing the answer.

***

Nina visited him that night. He lay alone in his bed. She slipped in with him. Like most Men, he slept naked. Her fingers explored him, and drew his own hands to her.

"I thought the Empress talked to you about this," he informed her. There was no moon, no light. In the darkness, he only knew her by the smell of her, by the softness of her skin, and the taste of her lips on his, as they were as soon as he spoke.

She pulled away. "I serve the Empress," she said, "but I'm a woman, too. I've given them over a dozen years – I have a right to a few moments in return."

She wrapped her legs around his – he felt her warm desire against him. Even as he knew where this was leading, this was his first time, and he didn't know if he wanted it to be with the Emperor's Watch Bitch.

Mistress of Pain.

"Are you always so forward?" he asked her, as she buried her head against his neck, her hot kisses on his skin.

"Never," she said. "Not once, not even thought of it. But I know you, Eric of Myr. I've known you my whole life, I think. Aschire women pick their mates when they meet them, and I think the reason that I could find no peace in the Aschire forest is that I had to meet you."

What a wonderful thing to believe, Eric thought. Lovers intentioned by the gods, drawn to each other across such voids.

Ashes in Eric's mind – he couldn't stop thinking of Tezzen being dead on the field, his friends, the boys and men that he'd grown up with and trained with, lying next to him. Bold Ayrak, shy Dev, laughing Kereck of the nine fingers.

He couldn't help thinking of the women in the camp, their bloody hands, their bloody faces, more like animals than women, literally tearing six rapists to pieces.

All of that, brought to his Volkhydro by the greed and the rage of an Emperor.

She took him in hand – his body responded whether his mind would or not.

"I'll love you, Eric of Myr," she promised. "Aschire mate for life – we have no others. Our children will be strong, the first of their kind, fair and powerful."

He took her by the hair. She whimpered, pressed her cheek into his palm. He held her eyebrows to his, felt her breath on him, strained to see her in the dark.

"Volkhydrans are conquerors and heroes, Nina," he informed her. "Would you be conquered? Would you be the prize of a hero?"

"I'll be whatever you want, Eric," she told him, breathless in his grasp.

He threw her down on her back, rolled on top of her. As he'd seen warriors do in the field, he took her, she gasping underneath him. He felt the sweet bite of her nails in his back, her teeth sinking into his shoulder. He slipped a hand under the small of her back, pinned her head to the mattress by her hair, and crushed her underneath him without mercy or thought of anything but his own pleasure.

As the dawn arose, red and angry, it found the two of them together, twisted in the bedding, her virgin blood on the sheets and both of their bodies. She slept in his arms, her hand on his bloody member, a smile on her lips as she snored softly.

He hadn't slept a wink – he had a decision to make. He could use Nina – she could get him audience with the Emperor. It would cost her – Lupus would know why he had done it, and how. She'd be disgraced, because she'd given her body to one who had no intention but to use her as a stepping stone.

His mother had suffered that. In the end of things, it had destroyed her. He might be the son of Lupus the Conqueror, but he was *not* his father's son.

He'd go with Vulpe and take his woman with him, and he'd find the Emperor in his own time.

Chapter Twelve:

From the Land to the Sea

Eric sold his string – he wouldn't need them in Andoron. In fact, his kinsmen were developing quite an affinity for horses.

Surrounded by Eldadorian Regulars, Vulpe became a different person. More confident, more in charge, more like a man and less like a child. Even Eric found himself wanting to call him 'Sir.'

He didn't, though. He wouldn't. Not his younger brother. He'd been offered a commission with the Regulars and dismissed it. He took on the position of advisor, of which the Prince had many – most of them friends of the Emperor.

Before Lupus had become an Emperor, or a Duke, or an Earl, he'd been Daff Kanaar – in Uman that meant Free Legion, a group of allies associated with each other out of their own desire as free people, not because they had to. They marked themselves with hook symbols on their breasts, topped with a dot. Karel of Stone had one so did Thorn, the Andaron of the Hunter tribe. Both accompanied Vulpe on his personal flagship, *The Dark Maiden,* just as Eric did.

He'd never been onboard a ship before, not even a river barge. There was something about the moving water – some message that it had for him. He felt as if, should he follow it, he'd be swept away and never find his way home.

Maybe that was the way of it. Stepping on that swaying deck, his mother gone, his friends dead by the hands of a father that didn't know him, he certainly felt like this was his last time in Volkhydro – like this was a chapter that had been closed in the story of his life.

He could see the tide was going out as the Regulars pulled the ship's lines in and dropped her sails. The ship inched out from the pier, leaving a crowd watching on the wharves, loved ones and well-wishers. The Empress Shela Mordetur stood among them, waving to her son and to her good friend and former nanny, Nina of the Aschire, Eric's woman now.

Nina pressed her body to his side and kissed his ear. She was elated to have found her man, to begin this new adventure with him. Eric felt full of ashes now. He knew what would be coming and he didn't feel like she should be a part of it, but he didn't see any other way either.

He wanted to face his father. That meant that he had to come to him through his family, and that meant that he needed to go through Vulpe. There was simply no other way.

"You're pensive," Nina commented to him, and bit him gently on his earlobe. Eric smiled despite himself. He put his arm around the girl, pulling her into his furs.

"It's been a long day," he said, "and I've never sailed before."

"I panicked the first time I saw the shore sink behind us, past the horizon," she told him. "Suddenly I was lost – I couldn't decide where the land was."

Eric nodded – he could understand that. Already, the ship had pulled out from the docks and was maneuvering around the 'breakwater,' a low wall out toward the sea, built to break the waves and make the harbor still.

A breakwater left the harbor more navigable, Eric thought. He could use one for his mind.

"Would you rather go below decks?" she asked him.

"No," he told her. "I want to see the sun."

"You could have me," she said, and kissed his neck. "We'd be all alone."

He smiled. He'd had her, he'd never experienced anything so amazing, so completely enveloping of his body and his mind. Not just the physical act, but the explosion of emotions, the look in Nina's eyes, her complete love and trust for him, as her man, who'd care for her and love her.

It was an amazing joy and an amazing commitment, and it was all swirling in his mind.

"I'll have you soon enough," he informed her. He could see her pouting without looking at her. "I'm surprised the Emperor didn't see us off."

"He did," she informed him.

"What?"

She pointed past Shela, at the head of the pier, at a crowd of Wolf Soldiers. Among them, one taller than the rest, with blond hair like his own, flowing past his shoulders.

He stood with his warriors, watching silently in his armor. That hook symbol in black, on his chest, the mark of the Daff Kanaar, visible even from this far.

How had he missed the Emperor? He could have spoken with him right then!

He knew better, though. There were the Wolf Soldiers guards to get past. No, he'd have to be introduced to his father, not announce himself.

His original plan had been foolish.

Eric of Myr wasn't going to be a fool.

***

The ship rolled across the waves, her masts tall and proud, her sails snapping like crossbow bolts in the wind, her pennons proclaiming her identity to the world. Dolphins leapt over her wake, her armada flowed out in a 'V' behind her.

Eric awoke in the morning from a sleep that had been amazingly peaceful. Nina had been insatiable, closer to him than his own skin. He'd collapsed exhausted into his narrow bed with her naked at his side, her nose in his neck, her hair across his face. The waves had rocked him afterward like his mother to its breast, and he'd descended into an exhausted, spent peace. When he arose with a warm woman and a full bladder, he was so completely refreshed that it surprised him.

He pushed up from the bed, Nina murmuring behind him. The dawn light was week in the hold, shining down the hatches to the decks. Warriors lay upon the floor around him, separated by curtains if at all, the more senior among them in hammocks. A few others were paired – the Regulars used both women and men. In general people kept to themselves.

No one had challenged them or interfered with them last night. They clearly feared Nina – she had a reputation that Vulpe had touched on. Word of Eric's treatment of the rapists back in Volkhydro had been whispered around, but it was a flicker to Nina's candle. It kept warriors from bothering with him.

He ascended to the weather deck, the salt air fresh in his face, and walked to the stern. The deck swayed beneath him, sailors in the rigging watching him, scowling. The ship's cooks were up already, cooking up a gruel in the fo'csle for when the warriors were roused. They'd exercise in the waist of the ship, then lay about all day.

It would take them a week to cross the Bay. They were four days into that. They'd land between the cities of Talen and Chatoos, make a base camp and then move east, destroying anything in their way.

Eric stepped up to the stern railing and lowered his pants. Darkening in the woodwork showed that he wasn't the only one who did this. Watching the dolphins, he relieved himself and sighed.

"You know," he heard behind him, "there's a belief that if you piss on a dolphin, you'll be blessed by Water for a month."

"I didn't think that Water blessed anyone," Eric said without turning. "The goddess sleeps wounded in her husband's arms."

Karel of Stone stood up next to him, dressed in bearskins turned inside-out, with a silver hook-symbol on his breast. He kept a sword over his shoulder, much as Eric did, and had the same blue eyes. A Scitai, he was a giant among them at three feet, two inches tall.

He seemed always to be smiling – he was no different now. It seemed that Karel found the rest of the world funny, but he was the only one who got the joke.

"She birthed Life," Karel pointed out. "Personally, I don't think she's unconscious; just quiet. That's the quality that makes her a goddess."

Eric chuckled. "You better hope she's sleeping, with that disrespect."

"Either I'm right or she'll never know," he said. Eric couldn't fault the logic.

He finished and cinched himself up. One look told him that Karel had come for the same reason – Eric turned and put his elbows on the rail.

"You're not original Daff Kanaar," Eric commented.

Karel didn't miss a beat, as Eric had expected. This man was a veteran, a warrior and a thief, and he'd probably seen enough in his life that this didn't surprise him. "The Daff Kanaar were already successful and well known when I joined them," he said. "They'd had a friend of mine named Drekk, an Uman, who'd died. I stepped in, took over, and eventually I was also Daff Kanaar."

"What does that symbol mean?" Eric asked.

"You're not afraid of a few direct questions," Karel commented, making a face.

"Not telling me?" Eric asked, after a long silence.

"Not sure," Karel said. "We pretty much keep our secrets."

Eric nodded.

"I can tell you that you don't choose the Daff Kanaar," Karel said. "The Daff Kanaar chooses you. You don't put that symbol on your own chest, you don't pick the color. Woe to them as have tried."

"Been a few?" Eric asked him, trying to be nonchalant.

"Been two," Karel answered him, send a high yellow arc over the stern. "And you don't want to know their fate."

Eric nodded.

"You look familiar to me," Karel said, finally. "Do I know your father?"

"If you do," Eric answered, as he always answered, "I'd thank you for an introduction."

"Oh," Karel said, and turned, leaning on the rail with his hands over his head, his forearms on the banister.

Eric sighed. "My mother is the daughter of a brewer in Myr," he said. "I own that now, since she died. I'd tell you that I'm a Viscount in Myr, but supposedly my lord, Tezzen, is dead, so I might be as much as a Count, now."

"Your Magnificence," Karel smiled and nodded to him.

Eric chuckled. You couldn't not like Karel of Stone, he thought. He was just too... himself. Karel seemed to be one of those individuals who reveled in the way Life made him.

"What was your mother's name?" Karel asked him.

"Aileen."

"Aileen of Myr?"

"Yes."

Karel looked sideways at Eric. Clearly *that* had gotten to him. "Small woman," he said. "Blond, kind of sad?"

Eric nodded.

Karel chuckled. "I knew your mother, and this might surprise you, but in fact we've met."

Eric turned toward Karel and leaned his elbow on the rail. "We have?"

He searched his memory, but he could remember no Scitai.

Karel nodded. "You weren't even three," he said. "I had business in Myr – your grandfather was an excellent brewer, and we Scitai love our beer. Many of the Daff Kanaar have their own side-businesses, and I am an importer/exporter."

"So you bought our beer," Eric said.

"I still buy it," Karel said. He stood straight, moving away from the rail. "Your mother had the same questions for me – do you know that?"

"Really?"

Karel nodded. "She asked me what the symbol meant, and for the look in her eyes – Eric, I have met with paupers and Kings, and no one but you mother has ever wrung an answer from me. I admitted to her – I didn't know."

"You don't know?"

Karel shook his head. "Then I found out from other members of the Daff Kanaar that *they* didn't know. Adriam himself sent them the symbol, and no one but Lupus knew what it meant."

"Why Lupus?" Eric was intrigued now – *this* was the sort of information he'd been craving.

Karel shrugged. "He looked at the rest of us, as if we were crazy, and he said, 'It's the answer.'"

"What?"

Karel nodded. "Now, that's what *I* said. 'What answer, Lupus?' I asked him."

"What did he say?"

Karel smiled. "He said, 'Karel, *that's* the question.'"

Eric knitted his eyebrows and pulled back his head.

"You're kidding with me," he accused the Scitai.

"Eveave render me a pauper," he said, putting a hand on his heart. "Lupus said those very words, and even the Uman-Chi among us couldn't gainsay him."

"So you're saying…" Eric wracked his brain.

He didn't like it – but that made a lot of sense to him. The symbol was out there – if you knew what to ask yourself, you'd look to it, and you'd say, 'Of course – that's been it all along!'

"I'm saying," Karel finished for him, "that Lupus the Conqueror doesn't think like anyone else, except for two people, and your mother was one of them."

"My mother?"

"I returned to Myr, and I told her that, and she looked at the symbol and said, 'Yes, I get that now.'" Karel informed him.

Then he reached out, and he placed a hand on Eric's upper arm, and looked into his blue eyes with his own, and he said, "And I think that, in time, you're going to get it, too.

"And probably for the same reason."

Eric didn't know if he liked that answer, but it was the only one he had.

Chapter Thirteen:

Landfall

It ended up taking eight days for the Sea Wolf armada to make landfall on the shore of Andoron. The day before they landed was Vulpe's birthday, and the whole armada celebrated it in the Bay. It made more sense than pitching some sort of bloody battle on it.

As it turned out, they might not have worried. The armada anchored off of the Andoron shore without so much as a single rider challenging them. Vulpe established a perfunctory beach head and then set his warriors to debarking and creating the jess doonar fit for his thousands.

Eric was among the first to debark, with Nina at his side. She kept looking to the East, as if she expected her kinsmen to show up and to welcome her.

"You miss your people?" Eric asked her. They stood on the plains, the long grass flowing like a great, yellow sea to their south.

She pressed her body up against his. The weather was perfect here – they didn't need warm furs, neither were they sweating. She reached up and kissed his cheek – even in the time that he'd known her, he'd grown taller.

"I'd love to see some of them again," she said. "It's been years since I've seen any from my own tribe, almost a year since I'd spoken Aschire with any other. I love the Emperor's family and have no regrets for my vows…"

"But family is," Eric finished for her. You could end that any way you wanted to, but your family existed, and there could be no replacement for them.

All of Eric's, of course, were dead.

Nina's problem was one of geography.

A jess doonar, as Eric learned, consisted of earthen walls and timber palisades, containing tents and cook fires, interspersed with storage, smiths, corrals and training areas. Everything that a warrior could want existed in the jess doonar, yet it could be defended against ten times the number of warriors protecting it and expect to stand.

Eric didn't see it – it made no sense. He could imagine himself with an invading army, coming across this thing on the plains. He'd bypass it, leave scouts, come back when they were leaving or wait for them to come after him. The Volkhydran in him told him that he had to fight an enemy if he came across one, and that angry part of his mind agreed, however there was a more rational part of him that knew that this was a trap, and the only way to avoid the trap was not to spring it.

"Nina!" he heard from behind him. "Eric! There you are!"

Vulpe was surrounded by his Majors and Colonels. He'd brought fifteen Millennia with him – in the Eldadorian Regulars, as with the Wolf Soldiers, warriors were broken into squads of ten, each squad having a sergeant. Ten sergeants reported to each lieutenant, five lieutenants to each captain, two captains to a major, who ruled a Millennia. When more than three Millennia were involved, then there would be colonels for each three, or divided between the Millennia, and the colonels reported to Vulpe.

Very symmetrical, very easy to understand. Vulpe relayed orders to five subordinates, and in moments it spread through not just through his whole army, but through the parts of the army that he wanted it to go to. Not only that, but the divisions gave more leverage to commanders on the ground, so that if he needed two hundred to take a ridge, then he relayed the order to a colonel, who then went to a major on the field, who decided *which* two hundred warriors to send, based on his situation.

Wolf Soldiers and now Eldadorian Regulars could win battles where they were horribly outnumbered. At the battle of the Foveans, as few as 25,000 Regulars crushed as many as 100,000 foreign warriors, under the leadership of the Hero of Tamara, a Volkhydran warrior.

"I'm having my pavilion set up at the center of the jess doonar," he said. "I want your tent beside it. The major here will see to it."

Vulpe nodded to an Uman. He didn't trust their kind, generally. Uman lived longer than Men and spoke a different language. They were common in Sental and Eldador, but they didn't think like Men, didn't act like Men. Men and Uman couldn't interbreed.

"Major Keffar of Uman City," he said. "I've been with the Regulars since the days of Glennen."

He extended his hand. Eric took him by the wrist, feeling the dagger up his sleeve. It wasn't uncommon for a military man to hide a weapon there. They released. He turned his attention and nodded to Nina.

"I've known this one since she was a girl," he said. "First time I ever saw her away from Lee's side."

Vulpe frowned. "I don't suppose she needs to be there now," he said.

All of the colonels and majors frowned. "My apologies, of course, your Highness," Keffar said. "What happened to your sister – the Trenboni will remember the day that we return to their city."

"More blood for blood," Eric heard himself saying. He caught himself, looking around him to the eyes on him.

"That I'll help you see to," he said to Vulpe. The younger man smiled.

"But this for now," he said. "Has Daggonin showed his face yet?"

Another colonel shook his head. "We beat him here," he said. "His 35,000 from Uman City will give us what we need – "

"No," Vulpe said, and started walking, the rest following him. Eric looked into Nina's eyes. She took him by his upper arm and they followed as well. "We have a lot more to do than just wait for numbers. We'll face Andaron horse; we need more than just hands on swords."

"Of course, your Highness," the colonel informed him.

"I want patrols out on the plains," he said. "I know my mother's people – there are probably a dozen eyes on us, and by the end of this week, there'll be one hundred more."

"We'll never catch them," another of the majors said.

"I know," Vulpe agreed. "But we can move them farther out. We'll need to trade with them and get horses and beef."

"We're invading – they'll trade with us?" Eric asked. That made no sense to him.

Vulpe chuckled. "We're invading the cities," he said. "The clans hate the cities. The cities hate the clans. We can invade the cities as much as we want – the clans won't care until we don't give them back, and then it will be too late."

"Which is why you don't want them to see our numbers," Eric said.

"Exactly," Vulpe agreed. "First Millennia, make it happen."

"Aye, Sir," another Major said. He turned on his heel.

The rest of the afternoon went like that – Vulpe giving orders, the officers carrying them out. It didn't take Eric long to realize that what he first thought of as the boy's brilliance was a check list that he'd memorized. Someone had trained Vulpe and drilled him, but he had learned the methods, not the lessons.

Vulpe was going to do very well until he came across a situation that he hadn't been drilled on – then it was going to be all him, and who knew how that would go?

Chapter 14:

Visitors

Eric sat his Andaron mount, watching Nina on the plains. She smiled as much as she ran, and she never tired of running. She moved almost with dance steps through the waving hay. Eric felt the grin on his own lips as his eyes followed her.

The mount had cost him three gold coins – a respectable price for an unshod animal. They'd been here for four days and, as Vulpe had predicted, the tribes were doing as much business with them as they could. They were hungrier for Eldadorian products than they were for gold; steel, saddles, files, pots and armor. Andarons lived free on the plains, but they still appreciated a good sword or a fine cast iron pan.

South of their jess doonar, Eric watched them, even farther south, watching him, watching Nina, watching the other tribes leading strings of horses and beef aurochs to the north. Nina would look up occasionally, look into strange Andaron eyes, maybe even share a word or two. Aschire and Andarons were not friends, but anyone could be cordial if the trade was good enough.

That angry voice in Eric's head actually chuckled now, appreciating the nature of Vulpe's trick. He'd build his strength on

Andaron goods, then use it to conquer the Andarons. By the time they realized their own mistakes it would be too late.

No charge of Theran Lancers this time. Eric might have liked to see that – the bold Therans against the wild Andarons, lances against arrows. It wouldn't be, though. He'd talked to Eric about that. The lancers would be dead on the plains, riddled with arrows on their horses. No, Eldadorian foot troops and their shields were the best way here.

Four riders separated themselves from one tribe and rode toward him. Eric watched four young girls, Vulpe's age, three sitting mares and one a stallion. They rode bareback with rope reins, one of them, not the one with the stallion, carrying a staff with a gem in it.

Eric focused on the staff – he'd heard of that. Certain wizards and sorceresses would force a sapling to grow around a gem and mix two aspects of Earth together, creating a staff of great power. This was extremely difficult to do – the tree would usually just bend and not embrace the gem. The staff at its more critical stages could require daily attention, and one mistake wasted the effort.

The staff meant something – he just knew it. Nina was watching the girls now, moving quietly toward him, her bow ready. Two of the girls carried long, Andaron throwing spears, they followed behind the girl with the staff, who followed behind another one, with no visible weapons.

She looked Eric in the eyes as she approached. His mind swam at the thought of the staff – he didn't know why. That same part of his brain that could be so angry was intense now, and its focus almost overwhelmed him.

"Oseeyo," the girl said to him, raising her right hand, palm out. Eric spoke Uman and the language of Men, and of course Volkhydran, which was similar, but not Andaron.

"Do you speak my language?" he asked, in the language of Men.

The girl smiled. "Of course," she said. "Hello, north man."

"Hello, south girl," he answered back. "You're bold ones, to be away from your tribe."

"My sister," she said, indicating the girl with the staff, "told me that we needed to meet you. She has the gifts, so we decided to come see what there was to see."

"I am Eric," he said, and raised his hand up, palm out, to show that he had no weapon.

"Waya Daganogeda," she said. "And my sister, Chesswaya. Our friends, Thorna and Nanette."

Eric nodded. "Wolf song," he said, "and... Wolf Bird?"

The one without the spear smiled. "I thought you spoke no Andaron," she said.

"I know a few words," Eric admitted. In fact, he'd heard the Empress refer to her husband as Yonega Waya – white wolf. After that, Vulpe had taught him some words and phrases.

"You come to trade?" he asked. Nina stepped up to his stirrup now, taking his lower leg in her hand. She'd nocked an arrow in her bow, but pointed the arrow down. Her message to these people: she wouldn't trust them, no matter how good the trade.

"Actually," she said, "we heard that Agtani Chewla was here, and we wanted to hear his song."

"You think he'll just sing for you?" Eric asked them. He doubted that they'd get within one hundred feet of Vulpa.

"We hear he sings all the time," Chesswaya said, "so we decided to just wait."

"They lie," Nina said. All eyes turned to her.

"Another sorceress," Chesswaya noted, "and a gifted one."

"More so than you, child," she said.

"Only one Aschire was ever trained in the arts," Waya Daganogeda said. "That woman is Nina of the Aschire, who protects the children of the Emperor."

Nina nodded.

"Then you'll bring us to the camp yourself, Nina," she said, "and introduce us to Agtani Chewla yourself."

"And why would I do that?" Nina asked them.

One of the other girls, Nanette, straightened up and said, "Because my uncle Thorn is in that camp, and he would want to see the daughters of Nantar of the Daff Kanaar."

***

People called Nantar of the Daff Kanaar the greatest warrior who'd ever lived. Heavier and yet shorter than the Emperor, black hair and black beard and forearms thicker than most Men's legs, if ever there was a true son of Volkhydro, then it was Nantar.

Eric had heard rumors that Nantar was with the rest of the Daff Kanaar, involved in the rebuilding of Luparran. His daughters were fostered by his best friend, Thorn, and Thorn's people, the Hunter tribe.

Thorn had come with Vulpe. He was a pinch-faced, dour Man with brown hair and brown eyes, who always saw a reason to frown. When the girls saw him, they leapt from their horses, and Thorna and Nanette ran to him.

He picked one up in each arm and smiled. They hugged him around his neck. Eric noted that, where the other girls wore dresses, these two worse pants and vests like boys, even though one of them was already showing a woman's form.

He dropped them, and regarded them with an expression already turned sour. "I left girls, I come back to warriors?" he demanded of them. "I promised your father that the Andarons would make women of you."

"And Shela told you that the Andarons would make us worse," Thorna scolded him. "You should have listened to her."

Thorn shook his head, then looked past the two girls to Waya Daganogeda and Chesswaya. "Who are these?"

"Our friends," Nanette introduced them. "Chesswaya has the gifts."

"I see the staff – who gave you that?"

"A warlord named Geeguh Digatish," Chesswaya said. "He was going to throw it away – he said it made him sick."

Thorn turned to Karel, standing next to him. He'd gotten his share of hugs already. "Geeguh Digatish is the warlord of Chatoos," he said.

"I know it," Karel informed him.

"I hardly think that's a coincidence," Thorn said.

Karel shrugged. "Everyone knows who you are, and what tribe you're from," the Scitai said. "If this was a message, it was a stupid one."

"Doesn't mean it wasn't a message."

Eric watched this. He took the staff and felt it, then handed it back to the girl. Eric burned to hold that staff – as if it held some secret for him.

Nina had remarked on it to him, but he couldn't discuss it. It went beyond words – there was something about this staff that he needed to know, but he didn't even know what it was.

No matter what, these girls bore watching.

Chapter Fifteen:

Introductions

The lights from the camp fires had burned low, only the crickets and the night birds were making any noise on the plains. Vulpe stood in the center of the jess doonar, ringed with Wolf Soldier guards, one of them a huge Dorkan, and another a skinny Uman.

He wore leather pants and a black doublet, open at the chest. He held his left hand in his right before him, his head down. Around him, thousands of warriors and Andaron visitors waited breathless – some of them had heard this before and some of them had heard *of* it.

He looked up, he smiled, and he opened his mouth to sing.

The Battle of Tamaran Glen, the popular song of how his father had led the Daff Kanaar to beat thirty thousand Confluni warriors with just two hundred Wolf Soldier guards and 4,000 Daff Kanaari mercenaries.

Eric could see the battle in his mind, his father waiting in the woods on his white stallion, the Confluni rolling like a living sea, breaking on the rock-hard savagery of Wolf Soldier resistance, Daff Kanaari warriors reaching around the Wolf Soldier shoals to strike and kill. Over and over, the Confluni dying, screaming, spattering their blood; swords clashing, scraping on armor, rending flesh. Eric's Volkhydran blood boiled, the song sweeping him away.

And then – the crescendo, the attack by arrows, Daff Kanaar warriors screaming, the Empress Shela Mordetur, then a pregnant slave, sweeps the Confluni archers away, and her master, Rancor Mordetur, sees her fall, struck down by magic.

Half the camp cried out in rage! Eric shuddered to realize that he'd been among them. Vulpe sang of the terrible Lupus, his charger flying through the woods, leaping into the Confluni army. The Emperor, then a Duke, cut a bloody swath with his sword, turning the ground red around him, weapons cleaving at his armor, warriors screaming in terror at his wroth. Lupus the Conqueror, the legend born, his rage, his grief, his woman and his child believed dead, trying to kill himself, trying to kill his enemies, the son of the god War, unleashed in his full fury!

Vulpe's voice rose and fell like that swinging sword, climbing higher, ever higher, telling of the Wolf Soldiers and the Daff Kanaari who saw him, screamed for him, raged with him, and joined him, impossibly outnumbered, leaping at the Confluni, tearing at them, beating them, crushing them.

Then Lupus through the fray, charging out the other side, clambering with his wounded stallion over the battered walls of the jess doonar and the bodies of the fallen from two armies to find his Shela, his slave, the mother of his child, the love of his life.

Vulpe's voice rose to that amazing peak, booming from a body that should be too small to accommodate it, then falling like a swooping falcon, to a hush so low that they strained to hear it, telling of the woman's sweet breast that rose, then fell, and told the warrior that, in fact, like himself, his woman and his child had survived.

Eric fell back on his heels, the energy sapped out of him. He could see it all. The tears on Lupus' rent face, where he'd received the scar known as the Mark of the Conqueror, mixing with blood, fell to Shela's breast in Eric's mind. Eric saw his invincible father in his vulnerability, as every warrior on the field had, then shook himself to realize that he'd been sitting on the plains quiet for minutes.

Then realizing that his own cheeks were wet with tears. Looking guiltily to either side, he wiped them away on his sleeve.

"Amazing," the woman, Waya Daganogeda, called 'Dagi,' said, next to him. She'd remained standing, watching Vulpe, watching all of them. She'd come here to witness this, to know the magic, to study the power. Her sister, Chesswaya, leaned on her staff, her head down, the gem in that staff pulsing green.

That staff – the new, angry side of his mind kept reminding him of the staff. The staff was a message, the staff was some sort of clue, some sort of sign. He'd found the girl with it, and he must know more about her.

Nina made that difficult. She didn't like other women around him, especially not women of the race of Men. She was jealous. She'd been a guardian too long and it colored her thoughts. Standing at his other side, she'd heard Vulpe sing this song and others many times. It wasn't that it didn't affect her; she just knew what to expect.

Eric pushed himself back up to his feet. His half brother was chatting with Thorn of the Daff Kanaar. Eldadorian Regulars were stirring now, going about their business, smiling and commenting to each other. Eric moved toward Vulpe, the four Andaron girls and his woman, Nina, with him.

"You amaze me with that," he said to Vulpe.

Vulpe smiled wide. "It's good for the warriors," he said. "They like it when I sing of a battle before an actual fight. It makes them dream of the troubadours who'll sing of their deeds."

Eric nodded – that made sense. Every warrior wanted to be a legend, the one who changed the world, the one who fought bloody on the side of a fight that won the day and then collected all of the swooning virgins.

"That song is hard for me now, though," Vulpe admitted.

Eric nodded. Vulpe hadn't spoken of it, but he'd loved his sister and he grieved for her. The Emperor was a cruel taskmaster and didn't relent against the enemy who had taken his daughter. In fact, it seemed to have renewed his efforts.

"I'm sorry, Chewee," Eric said. He reached out his hand and took Vulpe's wrist in his. It meant something different for him – this was his brother, and he felt that more keenly now.

Nina watched them both. She must be grieving, too, Eric thought, but she wouldn't talk of it. She seemed solely focused on him now.

"Your power amazes me, your Highness," Dagi said, stepping up to interrupt them. Vulpe released Eric and turned his attention to the girls. Even though Thorn vouched for them, the Wolf Soldier guards didn't take their eyes off of the girls. They were Andaron, and Vulpe was invading Andoron.

"Have you any other abilities, like your sister?" she pressed him.

"His sister is dead," the Uman Wolf Soldier snarled. "You'll show some respect."

"In fact, she's lost," Vulpe said, "not dead. No Mordetur is considered dead until you see the body, Grelt."

"Of course, Vulpe," he said. Eric was surprised by that – what subordinate called his superior by his given name?

"To answer your question," Vulpe said, to Dagi, "no, I'm not gifted like my mother, Nina and my sister. My singing is something that I do, but I don't exercise it like my sister's magic."

Dagi nodded. "My sister, Chesswaya," she said, "is gifted as well – she's very powerful, even without her staff."

"Your sister?" Vulpe asked her. All of the girls smiled.

"You notice that we're from different tribes," Dagi said, pulling at the hem of her dress. "Yes, I'm a Hunter, she's a Long Manes. My mother was a Wet Belly, and hers a Drifter."

"Both those tribes are dead," Thorn said.

"Because my father destroyed them," Vulpe said, looking into the girls' faces. "Is that why you're here? You want something because my father destroyed your tribe? Did he kill your father?"

Chesswaya smiled, then looked at the rest of them and lowered her head, batting her green eyes. Dagi kept her head high. "There is nothing wrong with our father," she said, "and he is not dead. Neither of us would ever think of getting vengeance from Lupus the Conqueror, nor from his son."

"Then what?" Vulpe demanded. The Wolf Soldier guards closed in a little. Eric could see the snare closing.

"As I said," Dagi told him, "we wanted to hear you sing. You're amazing."

Flattery, Eric thought. He wondered how that would work on the Prince.

It didn't. He just straightened. "Everyone knows how I sing," he said.

"But not everyone has heard you," Dagi argued. "I hadn't – we hadn't."

Vulpe looked into the faces of the Wolf Soldiers around him – he was used to getting advice from others, that much was clear. Finally Vulpe's eyes found his half-brother.

"What's your opinion?" Vulpe asked him.

The angry part of his mind had plenty of suggestions for him, but he already knew the answer. "Keep them close," he said. "Learn from them. Two of them belong here anyway – the other two bear watching."

Vulpe nodded. The girls exchanged glances but didn't seem about to run.

One of the Wolf Soldiers took Nanette by the upper arm – faster than Eric would have believed, she turned her arm and smacked him between the eyes with the back of her fist, then drove her heel into his knee, dropping him. Thorna spun on one heel and delivered a one-two punch into the face of the Wolf Soldier closest to her, placing her back to Nanette's.

Nina raised a hand glowing white with power. Chesswaya raised her staff and pointed it at Nina, and the white power died.

Eric already had his sword in his hand, although he didn't remember drawing it.

"Stop this," Vulpe ordered them. He didn't raise his voice, but he clearly asserted his will.

The Wolf Soldiers froze, the Eldadorian Regulars right after them. Dagi stood with her arms crossed under her breast, watching him with a smile on her face.

"Will you stay?" Vulpe asked her.

She looked around her, then nodded. "We appreciate the invitation," she said.

In his mind, that angry portion chuckled. Eric sheathed his sword.

'This,' he couldn't help thinking, 'was something.'

Chapter Sixteen:

Moving Forward

On the 3rd day of the month called Water, the scouts on patrol called the alarm that there were ships crossing the horizon to the north. They were, by definition, ten daheeri away, a daheer being one tenth the distance to the horizon. Almost an hour later, these ships were identified as Sea Wolves coming in from Uman City.

The reinforcements had arrived – and not one attack on the Eldadorian troops by the Andarons. Foveans in general were waiting for the Druid Dilvesh, called 'The Green One,' to speak before the Fovean High Council this month. No one was going to attack the Eldadorian Empire before that, for whatever reason.

Eric watched the huge three-masted vessels anchoring off of the Andaron shore. They were too huge to beach themselves and had no oars for backing out. They'd spend this day and the next, and possibly the one after that, ferrying their warriors to the shore, where they'd make a second and a third jess doonar, each a daheer apart.

"It's glorious, isn't it?" Nina asked him, standing with her body pressed to his side, her hand slid down the back of his fur leggings. They'd gotten themselves a tent, and if Nina had been inhibited in any way in the hold of the ship, then she was completely unrestrained now.

Either she wanted a child by him or she was making up for more than a decade of celibacy – either way Eric found himself between craving and dreading sleeping with her, for her demands on him and the way she made him feel with him in her arms.

"Glorious," he allowed. He didn't feel that way. He knew what these troops did in his native Volkhydro, and he dreaded what they'd perpetrate in Andoron.

"When Lupus came to the Aschire, he promised us that he would save us and, when he stood supreme in Fovea, we would be at his right hand," Nina informed him. "Now he's made it come to pass. When Andoron belongs to Eldador, there will be nothing left to threaten us."

"Except, of course, the Eldadorians," Eric said, still watching the ships.

He could feel her looking at his profile. Her beautiful gray eyes searched the side of his face.

"He would never let them," she murmured, but he didn't answer her.

He had other things on his mind.

***

"You're a quiet one," Eric heard from behind him.

Nina had gone out hunting. She'd invited him, but he wasn't in the mood for it. The Eldadorian army and what they were here to do made him feel dark inside, and this new, angry portion of his brain seemed to be thriving on it and adding to his general testiness.

"I don't speak unless I have something to say, Dagi," he said, without turning. He was sitting by a fire in the dawn light, waiting for a haunch to start popping so that he could carve it.

"Can we join you?" she asked him.

He pointed to the empty space next to him. "I don't like to eat alone," he admitted.

"Neither do we," he heard – that was Chesswaya. Like him, she was a quiet one.

They sat on either side of him, and quietly watched the fire popping. To the north, the Sea Wolves had already begun disembarking again. Over half their number had unloaded – the ships should be leaving today.

The warriors crowded the plains and devoured as much beef as the Andarons could sell them. They'd be eating their own reserves soon enough, but the longer those waited, the safer they were.

"Well, there's a picture," they heard from the other side of the fire. Looking across it, past the haunch on the spit, they saw Karel of Stone, the silver hook symbol almost glowing on the front of his bear skins.

He'd just appeared out of the dawn gloom – Eric knew that the Scitai moved like mice, being barely larger, so it couldn't be a surprise when one showed up out of nowhere, however it still unnerved him when it happened.

"Will you join us?" Dagi asked him.

He snorted and walked right to the fire's edge. "For beef and ale, the fare of Men?" he asked. "Too early in the morning for a belly ache and a hang over."

"As you will," Eric said, dismissing him.

Nina would return soon from the hunt. She'd join them and take over all conversations, probably with a million tales of the clumsiness of Men and the tedious caution of Uman, and how they'd spoiled her hunt. He'd hoped for a little quiet until then, but he'd settle for solemn Chesswaya and pushy Dagi without the constant joking of the Scitai.

"What – which are you?" Karel demanded, squinting through the fire. He straightened, then stood up on his tip-toes, then that smile returned.

"Eric," he said, that mocking smile back. "You fooled me, youngling."

"Who did you think I was?" Eric growled. If Karel wanted to insult him by calling him one of the women, he'd better be good with his sword.

"Truth be told," Karel said, "I'd thought I was seeing double, then triple, and *now* I think I just see one of the same, but in three different forms."

"Riddles, riddles," Dagi grumbled. She stood and turned the haunch so that the bottom side wouldn't burn. Eric had been about to do the same thing. She stretched across the fire – she'd be a beautiful girl, this one.

But not as beautiful as his Nina. No woman could *really* compare to Nina. Even the Empress' raw beauty paled beside her, as far as he was concerned.

Karel surprised them all by squatting down by the fire, opposite them. "Oh, it was a riddle, I think, but that's solved now," he said. "Now all I have to do is to decide what to do with it."

"What are you talking about?" Eric growled. That angry portion of his mind breathed caution at him now – this Scitai was of a very clever people, who acted clownish to put others off their guard. The Scitai might be speaking of riddles, but that might mean secrets, and there were secrets that Eric didn't want told.

Not until he was ready.

"He's crazy," Dagi grumbled, sitting back down.

"No," Chesswaya murmured, more to herself than to them. "He's wise, but he's foolish, too, because he thinks that being the smartest one at the fire makes the rest of us stupid."

"Is that it, Scitai?" Eric demanded of him. "Do you think me stupid? Do you think these girls are stupid?"

"No, no," Karel said, and held his hands out before him, to the fire. "But this morning I saw a thing that I didn't expect to see, and now I don't know what to do about it. Chesswaya calls me the smartest one at the fire, but I'm afraid that I'm the one who's only just learned what the three of you already know."

Eric looked to his left and his right, into the two girls' eyes. What could the Scitai be talking about? It made no sense – maybe this was some trick of his, to see if they even *had* any secrets to tell.

"I agree with Dagi," he said, finally. "He's crazy. I don't want to hear you anymore, Scitai. If you want to talk about secrets, Scitai, you'd better be telling one."

"Ok," he said. "Here's a secret for you."

Dagi leaned forward, Chesswaya just sat there, looking down at the staff in her lap. Eric straightened, not wanting to seem too eager, expecting another word game.

"You think the Emperor is making peace, and then you think the Emperor is making war under the cloak of peace, but in fact, you'd be wrong. The Emperor wanted an all-out brawl, and making peace is the only way that he can think of to get it."

'What was *that* supposed to mean?' Eric wondered. The Emperor had *been in* an all out brawl with the Battle of the Foveans, where 25,000 warriors met another 100,000. If that wasn't an all-out brawl then what was?

What would it take to sate the Emperor's hunger for combat?

Dagi shook her head and leaned back down. Chesswaya looked up, smiling.

"That wasn't a secret," she said. "That was on the wind. Anyone could know that. Do you want to hear a *real* secret?"

"Chessa..." Dagi warned.

"Please," Karel informed her. "I'd like to hear a real secret."

"You know that thing that you think only you know of, that put that mark on your chest?"

Now she had Karel's attention.

"Before this war is done, not only won't you have it, you won't be free of it, and you'll be wondering *what* is keeping it."

Karel looked down, then looked back up, and his smile was gone. Eric turned to look at Chessa's profile, wondering what was going through the young girl's head.

"I don't think I liked that secret," the Scitai said, finally.

Chesswaya chuckled, and Dagi stood with a dagger to cut the haunch. She offered a strip to Eric, as the nearest male, then to Chessa, because Karel had said he didn't want any. The Scitai just sat there, quiet, thinking of Chesswaya's secret.

No matter what else happened, Eric thought, chewing his beef, this wasn't going to be a good day.

***

Afterward, looking out to the Bay, watching the ships deliver soldiers to the shore, Eric spoke with Nina about what he'd heard from Dagi and Chesswaya. The two girls were with Thorn, now – he wanted them to practice their riding and their archery while he had them with Nanette and Thorna.

"That's not a good conversation," Nina said, finally. "I think that we need to talk to Vulpe about that, and then he should talk to his mother as soon as he can."

"You don't like those girls," Eric accused her. She looked into his eyes.

"No," she said. "They're strange, even for Andarons. Andaron Sorceresses are powerful, and their tribes guard them. It's very uncommon for one to be out with no males to protect her. This

Dagi is like no Andaron I've ever seen – she's outspoken and she's strong, and Andaron like their girls meek.

"I wouldn't know," Eric admitted.   He hadn't met many Andarons.

"Well, take it from me, for strange girls, those girls are strange, and they were drawn right to Vulpe," she said.

Eric kept looking out to the water. He'd wondered about that, too, but lately it had occurred to him, and the angry part of his mind agreed:

Maybe it wasn't the Prince whom these girls were really here to see.

Chapter Seventeen:

On the Road

An army of one thousand can be on the move in minutes. Two thousand will take more, and if there are horsemen and lancers, the time is even longer.

Mercenaries can be quicker than regular troops – they're just more adept at getting out of wherever they are. Militia – troops raised to defend a besieged city or holding – take forever. Eric had seen two grown Volkhydrans fighting over a blue and a red doublet, each arguing for the red because he would look more fierce in it.

Vulpe's army ran fifty thousand strong, not just with warriors from every land but including horses and dogs as well. An army that large could only get moving in stages. If they'd even tried to just stand up and walk, they'd trample each other, and most would never be fed, while the rest would eat themselves senseless and be useless.

Fifty Millennia – ranks of one thousand warriors – were controlled by fifty Majors in the Eldadorian Regulars. These, in turn, answered to ten Colonels, who answered to Vulpe and three Generals.

One of these, supreme under Vulpe, Eric knew as Colonel Gartheld Daggonin. He dressed in Eldadorian greens with steel sleeves and leggings, a sword over his back. His white hair circled the bald spot on the top of his head. His full mustachios drooped two inches past the corners of his mouth. He had full lips and a ruddy nose, and his brown eyes kept the flat look of a Man who'd seen others die on the end of his sword.

Eric knew this Man as a Major – the one who'd been responsible for the fall of Volkha, and who'd been regent there after Vulpe's victory there. He'd ordered warriors slaughtered for doing as little as touching their weapons around an Eldadorian guard.

Eric looked him straight in the eye, Nina at his side, her body close to his. Daggonin held Eric's gaze unflinching.

"Do I *brhm-hrm!* know you, Volkhydran?" Daggonin asked, in front of Vulpe and a pavilion full of officers. "Is there maybe something you *brm-ha!* need to discuss with me?"

No doubting what that meant. Vulpe stepped right in. "I owe my life to this warrior," he said, "and he's with me, Colonel."

Daggonin looked away from Eric and down at Vulpe, not smiling. "You just made *brhm-hrm* war on these people," he said. "You have to expect they'll try something to get close to you."

"They did," Vulpe said, taking a step closer to Eric, exposing his young back to Eric's sword. The Colonel didn't miss it. "He's the one who saved me from them."

"If you're sure of him *brm-ha!*, I have no issue with him," Daggonin said, then turned his face back to Eric. "If he has no issue with me."

"He doesn't," Vulpe informed him.

"I didn't hear him *hrm* say that," the Daggonin challenged him.

Eric raised his eyebrows and looked at Vulpe. "You tolerate that?"

Vulpe smiled a half-smile. "My father encourages his Wolf Soldiers to be frank with him and to call him by his first name," he said. "It drives generals crazy all over Fovea, so I do it, too, to a degree. I'm not stupid – I know that he knows more about warfare than I do."

Daggonin smiled in Eric's face but didn't look away.

"No," Eric said, finally. "I have no problem with him. He did nothing to me or mine."

Vulpe nodded. A long table had been placed in the center of the pavilion, and a map laid down on it, with blocks down on the map. The blocks represented Millennia and how they'd be moved from here to Chatoos.

Vulpe and the General turned toward it, Eric and Nina behind them. Karel of Stone actually stood on the table, and Thorn waited with his arms crossed on the other side, the four young girls around him. Dagi stood to one side of him, her arms crossed over her breast, watching Vulpe and Eric. Dagi was an interesting girl with her own opinions. Nina had already made it clear that she hated the Andaron.

The Aschire tended to be jealous.

"We march for ten hours a day," said another General, Grak of Andurin of the race of Men, an Eldadorian son of the Duke Groff, gone to the Regulars for a military career. Like his father, he stood tall and thin, with straight hair down past his shoulders, brown showing a little gray. Like Daggonin, he dressed in Eldadorian greens with steel sleeves and leggings, and a thin sword on his hip.

"So we'll send out one Millennia an hour for ten hours, every day," he continued. "That means that we'll be five days apart from front to back – our first Millennia will arrive at Chatoos four days after the last leaves here."

Daggonin and Vulpe nodded, as did the other General, an Uman whom Eric hadn't met. "You'll be hard pressed for forage for the last ten," Thorn said. "No more Andarons are coming to trade with you – they're fat and happy now and run deep into the plains to be away from this mass.

"How are our supplies?" Vulpe turned his head to Major Keffar – as a native of Uman City, the Uman knew the most about the supply trains.

"Good, not great," he said. "We won't starve. Those Sea Wolves dragged nets here and collected a good bit of fish in addition to our beef and vegetables."

"Milk? Ale? Fresh water?" Grak asked of him.

Eric snorted. Milk? Milk spoiled in a day – what good was that?

"Weeks' worth," Keffar said, with a sideways look at Eric. "I think your young friend doesn't know the secret of storing milk."

All eyes turned to Eric, and he felt uncomfortable, but held himself straight. "You've learned how to store milk?" he asked.

"My father calls it 'past-izations,'" Vulpe said. "You treat the milk with boilings and spices, and it lasts even a month if you keep it cool. We have ice in wagons, and we'll drink milk."

Eric nodded appreciatively. Every farmer knew that milk made you strong – being able to give a luxury like that to his troops would give Vulpe a real advantage, especially against Andarons, who drank mare's milk and had a ready supply of it.

'Imagine that,' Eric thought to himself. These warriors weren't just banging their armor and sharpening swords – they were planning on feeding, on drinking, on moving. For the next hour, as troops were marshaled on the field with their orders to move, Eric learned that the actual fighting was, in fact, the smallest part of the war, and that the things that made for victory might pass even a week before the first two warriors crossed swords.

People wondered why the Emperor kept victory coming after victory. Hopelessly outnumbered but never out-matched, Rancor Mordetur might actually be winning for the simple reason that he was planning for his wins.

Eric felt an unfamiliar surge of pride and awe for his father. Nina looked up at the side of his face as he stood up a little straighter, thinking about whose blood flowed with his mother's in his veins.

His mother, sweet, dedicated Aileen, who'd believed unto her dying breath that she would return to Lupus' side.

Eric would talk to that man, but he wondered now if he wouldn't have a different conversation.

***

The second Millennia left right after dawn on the seventh day of Water, and Eric left with them, Nina sitting on the butt of his horse, her arms around his middle. Vulpe would leave during the day and catch up with them – dealing with more of the details of the move for as long as he could, instructing as well as learning. The second would normally have belonged to Major Keffar, however he needed to remain back and coordinate the supply train. Rather than trailing them from a drop point, the supplies would be embedded between the Millennia, and Eric had to assume that it was more difficult to keep it moving than it sounded.

Another Major, an Uman named Lek, rode a palomino gelding next to Eric. He'd been built spare like most Uman, long fine limbs and long, thin fingers, arched eyebrows and pointed, lobeless ears, one with a gold earring in the top. The Major seemed to be on the verge of saying something, but remained quiet for the first hour.

After that, he sighed and asked Eric, "Have we met, my Lord?"

Eric was about to remind him that he wasn't 'His Lord,' when he remembered a day, merely two months ago, when Tezzen had named him. Now dead, Tezzen might have left him a Count for all he knew – if he ever returned to Myr at all.

"I doubt it," he said. "I've only met Uman from Sental."

Lek nodded, looking forward, then sideways at him, then forward again. "I'd swear I've seen your face."

Nina gave him a squeeze and kissed his ear.

"I've dealt with that my whole life," Eric informed him. "The blonde hair is rare among my people, so if you see one, you think you've seen us all."

"That could be it, I suppose," the Uman said, but Eric didn't think he believed it.

He felt thin fingers on his scalp. "I love this hair," she said. "It's thick and long – you want to know what it has me thinking?"

"Maybe what you're always thinking?" Eric chided her.

The Uman snickered, then looked at Nina and stopped, looking straight forward. Nina might be playing at the loving wife now, but she'd been one of the most feared of the Emperor's vassals for more than nine years.

People don't forget a reputation like that.

Chapter Eighteen:

The Belly of the Beast

Eric had come to an important conclusion: he didn't like his new horse.

He'd given the beast three days, and every day the mount had gotten worse, not better. His trot felt like he was hammering nails. His canter was worse. When he walked he moved slower than a marching soldier.

He'd been cheated by the Andaron tribe – he knew they only traded the horses that they didn't want any more, but this animal should have been put down.

"You're tense, my love," Nina whispered into his ear, hugging him around his middle, sitting behind him on the saddle.

"I'm sick of this," he said. "We walk, we sail, we wait, we ride. You know what Volkhydran warriors do? They fight, that's what. When do we fight?"

He felt her cheek on his shoulder. "In good time, my love, in good time."

Eric already knew that answer – he'd seen it for himself. The preparation, the planning, all toward a single goal, all with a purpose in mind. The Empire didn't just strike at random – this was all according to a plan so intricate, with so many layers, that it moved almost on its own, as if it were an animal, as if her were in the belly of a beast, and the beast were moving, just carrying him along.

But the belly had become a cage, and the cage walls were tightening. They rode, they ate, they slept, they rode – every day the same, all things the same, because it worked, Eric knew, because this was the safe way, and the right way, and the sure path to victory.

The Emperor knew the way to win, and he'd taught it to his son, and his son would win – the enemy defeated before the battle began.

Where was the glory in that? Where was the challenge?

Where was the fun? How was a man to get his adrenaline up when he knew he'd be alive tomorrow?

Vulpe hadn't caught up with them yet – fast riders had informed them that he'd be with the second Millennia tomorrow. Eric knew that this could have been *his* Millennia, if he'd accepted a commission with the Eldadorian Regulars, but the idea turned his stomach.

He needed to be out of here. Eric of Myr had been born a Volkhydran, and no matter what the Empire might believe, Volkhydrans lived free.

"We're leaving," he informed Lek, riding next to him.

Lek shook his head. "You don't have permission."

"I'm not an Eldadorian and I'm not a Regular," Eric informed him. "I don't need permission."

"The Lord Supreme Commander gave me my orders –" Lek began.

"Are you ready to fight me?" Nina asked from behind him.

Lek looked behind Eric, then swallowed.

"Well?"

He shook his head.

"We're leaving," Nina informed him. "Let Vulpe know we'll be back."

"Yes, my Lady," Lek said. "Wouldn't you at least like an escort?"

"Do you think that I *need* an escort?" Nina asked him.

He looked away. Eric pulled the horse's reins to the left, turning him south.

He didn't like the idea of hiding behind a woman – however Nina had made herself *his* woman, and then any comment on him would be a comment on her.

Better not to comment on the Mistress of Pain.

The horse's terrible, rough gallop brought them south. Eric spent more time on the balls of his feet in the saddle, than he did in the seat. He rode cavalry – a high cantle and a front ridge, but no proper horn. The horse didn't like it – probably more used to a blanket.

The daheer passed with an agonizing slowness. He'd barely covered three before he found the first Andaron tribe. Nina had just clung to him the whole time, saying nothing.

The Andaron sat proud in the saddle, a chieftain among his people, his warriors back one hundred feet from him. He had long, brown hair with grey streaks in it, no shirt, leather leggings, no shoes. A bow hung from the saddle before him, his scimitar on a belt over his shoulder. His mustachios hung down past his chin – he hadn't been a war lord for more than a few years.

But this had been the Andaron whose tribe had cheated him.

"Oseeo," Eric greeted the man, in his own language.

"Oseeo," the war lord answered him, nodding.

"You know this horse?" Eric asked him.

"Everyone knows that horse," the warlord said. "It's been in more tribes than a *gadanahi gadayuchaw*."

"You call my horse a *gachway*?" Eric frowned at him.

The warlord had called the horse a 'dirty girl.' In the tribes, that would be a 'dirty girl,' a woman who'd been defiled, who was passed from tribe to tribe. No one would marry her – they'd feed her and use her and pass her on.

A 'gachway,' was a *yonega ukada* or 'white face' girl who sold herself for money. That was one of the most dire insults that an Andaron could deliver.

"I did not," he said, straightening. The Andarons had done a lot of trading with the Eldadorians. They knew how many warriors Vulpe had – they didn't want trouble.

Eric knew that a bad trade was all part of the game – that cheating was just another part of trading. He'd bought the horse too soon, amazed at his low price, and that would be on him.

Eric didn't feel like being reasonable. Eric felt like being a Volkhydran today and, sometimes, a Volkhydran had to fight.

The angry part of Eric's brain had been restless and irascible. Eric could feel it grinning at this now.

"Perhaps you think that this horse is your mother?" Eric asked the war lord.

Eric felt Nina's arms tighten around him. There wasn't an Andaron alive who wouldn't answer an insult like that.

The Andaron war lord screamed his challenge; Eric answered him with his Volkhydran war cry. The Andaron kicked his horse into motion, and Eric his.

Eric's horse snorted and shied. Nina leapt from its butt. The Andaron thundered toward him, moving with his horse, one being of two parts, stamping and snorting and swinging a scimitar. Even if Eric managed to get the horse under control, he'd never match the Andaron.

Instead he pulled his sword and smacked the horse in its flank with the flat of his blade. The horse reared, and Eric pushed off backwards from it, landing on his feet, then stepping back several steps to catch his balance. The rearing horse held up the charging warrior, Eric sprinted to its right side, to catch the Andaron on the left.

The Andaron leapt from his saddle as well. He wasn't honor bound to do it, but he likely wanted to show his warriors that he could defeat a yonega ukada boy without any advantages.

Eric felt the grin spread over his face. That would be a mistake.

The Andaron had his sword out – Eric did as well. The Andaron circled to his right, trying to get Eric to do the same, to open up is left, to give him a shot at his body. Neither warrior wore any armor – this was, as Volkhydrans described it, a fight between steel and skin.

The Andaron swung low, for the shin, met Eric's sword and turned his wrist, swinging high for the head, pulling the blow and going for a stab to the chest. Eric smacked the obvious attack aside and struck for the Andaron's groin.

The Andaron parried, but Eric turned his weapon in his grip, meeting the scimitar's edge with the flat of his blade. The weapon rang in the Andaron's hand, surprising him.

Eric had created this move on his own, out of his own head. The sudden 'bang' stunned his opponent, he whipped the sword over his own head and cleaved down at the Andaron's shoulder.

The Andaron parried just in time, Eric pressed down on the other's blade, pushing for the shoulder, surprising his opponent again. For a moment they stood there, man-to-man, straining, struggling, one warrior's strength against another.

Eric bore down on the other's weapon, applying his weight. The Andaron's knees started to buckle. The crossed blades inched closer to the neck, the shoulder.

Eric's hands, together on his weapon's hilt, slipped into the intricate basket. The black blade flashed all of its own.

The Andaron's blade shattered, almost exploding between them, as Eric drove his own weapon deep into the other's shoulder.

Deep into the rib cage, through the heart, and amazingly through the other side, actually cutting the Andaron warlord in half.

Blood flew as if from a fountain. Eric stepped back from his handiwork, seeing the warrior's shocked expression, frozen on his dead face. Eric had killed before, but he'd never done it like this, never gone out looking for a fight, demanding it like this.

It shocked him, twisted through him like a worm, leaving him cold and warm at the same time. He'd made a transition right then – he knew it. He used to be a warrior.

Now he was a killer.

Nina stood up next to him – she'd knocked an arrow in her bow. The Andaron warriors were approaching slowly, gathering their courage, perhaps?

"Take his horse," she whispered in his ear.

"What?"

Nina took him by the upper arm. "His horse – you came here because they cheated you for a horse, now you demand his horse in trade."

Eric looked into her beautiful gray eyes, so full of concern.

"If you came here to get even, then they'll let you go," she told him. "If you came here just to kill a man, then they owe you a blood debt."

Eric nodded. He stepped up to the Andaron's horse, standing sniffing at the dead man's blood, and took a fist full of mane. The horse started to balk, but Eric put a foot into the stirrup and hauled himself up into the saddle. He reached his foot into far stirrup as the horse circled, resisting the new riders.

Now the Andarons were closing, twenty strong, more farther back.

Nina leapt up behind Eric, making his horse balk. He pulled the reins to one side and turned the horse completely around, then faced the advancing Andarons.

"I was cheated," he proclaimed. "He paid the price. I'll take his horse and leave mine. Anyone who thinks they can take this horse from me, you step up now."

Their eyes shifted between Eric and the armed woman behind him, finally stopping at their horses. Andarons didn't like Aschire and they didn't trust Yonega Ukada, but they'd just seen this one humble their war lord, and if any of them could do that, then likely he would have that job.

Eric pulled back on the reins and backed the horse up. An excellent stallion and well trained, he obeyed instantly. When they didn't pull their bows, he turned the horse and kicked him in the ribs. He took off across the plains, back toward the Eldadorian army.

He knew he shouldn't but he felt a *lot* better.

Chapter Nineteen:

Another Path

The new stallion was superior – better than he'd ever ridden. Other warriors in the Millennia noted it immediately, a few of the Andarons commenting on it.

The fight replayed itself over and over in Eric's mind. He'd never done anything like that before – never just gone out looking for trouble and then not only finding it, but killing someone in the process.

Is this the man he wanted to become? Is this Aileen's son? He knew that he was behaving as most Foveans saw Volkhydran warriors and the race of Men in general.

Were they right?

"You're pensive, my love," Nina whispered into his ear, sitting behind him.

He felt her arms around his middle, her fingers slipping inside of his furs. He grinned to himself and leaned back against her.

"When are we supposed to arrive in Chatoos?" he asked her.

She stiffened. She'd been doing that. She wanted more conversation from him, more information about his feelings. It unnerved him. A man kept his feelings, or they changed how he behaved.

"The First Millennia should be there tomorrow," she informed him. "We arrive an hour after them."

Eric nodded. Vulpe had arrived with them the day before. He'd commented on the horse, but didn't say more. He didn't have to – the major, Lek, had made a full report according to Nina, who'd spoken with the Prince privately.

Eric was starting to feel like one of the Regulars. He ate with them, he rode among them. He hadn't taken a commission, but they acted as if he had.

"Signs of resistance?" he asked.

"Hungry for another fight?" she countered.

He might be, he thought. There could be a mindlessness to it – a single point of focus. With a sword in his hand, a foe in front of him, he didn't have to worry about the person he had been, the man he was becoming. He could focus on the problem, on staying alive, on being Eric, of Myr, son of Aileen.

Son of the Emperor of Eldador.

The idea filled him with rage.

"Off," he told her.

"What?"

"Off," he said, straightening. "Get off the horse."

"My, Eric, I…" she stammered.

She thought she'd offended him. She'd want to talk. She wanted to discuss his *feelings*, to understand what was in his heart.

But his heart had filled with bile, and he didn't like it, didn't deserve it. He'd come to face a man who'd fathered him, and to hold him accountable for his actions with his mother. Instead he was embroiled in a war, and on that warrior's side of it, and he was nowhere near this father.

Instead, he was helping his father's other son.

"Off," he roared, half-turning. "Get off! Get off! Get off! Get off! *Get off!*"

She pushed herself backwards, landing on her feet behind the stallion. The hurt look on her face was unmistakable.

He couldn't care about that now.

He whipped the stallion's behind with the reins. The beast leapt forward, powerful hind legs digging into the earth, Eric lurching back in the saddle. Marching warriors moving in perfect columns parted as the sixteen-year-old clapped his heels to the horse's sides and took off across the plains, his head down and a woman crying in his wake.

***

The stallion's hooves thundered across the plains, tireless and free, the boy on his back leaning forward, gripping the reins, tears flowing free down his cheeks.

He tried to tell himself that they were from the wind.

He remembered the expression on that dying man's face. He remembered the look of serenity on his mother's as well.

He could imagine how his friends and Tezzen must have looked, being left for the crows on the field of battle.

He didn't want to live that life. He didn't want to be the person who made that happen. He'd killed a man out of his own anger and for no other reason. He'd probably left a widow. He'd probably left orphans. He'd grown up thinking that he was one, but from a wealthy family. How would it be for these, living on the plains?

He didn't know. He didn't want to know. He didn't want to think about it. He urged the stallion on, running faster, its mane flying, its sides heaving, moving with it, becoming one, a streak across the plains.

The beast stumbled – he nearly fell across the front ridge. He reined in, catching himself, thinking, "You can't do this – you don't know the terrain here." One chuckhole or bad divot and the horse could break a leg. He'd have to kill it, another innocent on your conscience.

He'd be stranded. As the beast stopped, he looked over his shoulder, seeing that he'd already left his Millennium over the horizon. If he pressed on, he'd probably overtake the next one.

Maybe he should do that, he thought. Maybe he should spend some time with new faces. Nina would live without him for a while – it might even be good for her.

"You, there!" he heard to his left side.

He had his sword out before he thought about it. He turned the stallion to face the disruption, and saw a dozen Andarons rising up out of the hay around him. They'd laid their horses down when they'd seen him coming, and stayed hidden. It was just a coincidence that he hadn't ridden past him – perhaps they thought that he was on to them and had stopped because he'd detected them.

No chance they thought that now – he'd clearly been surprised. He sat the panting stallion, waiting. He had an excellent animal – he could run back to his Millennia if he had to.

He scanned faces – he didn't recognize them. He didn't think that this was the tribe he'd traded to, the one whose war lord he'd killed. It wasn't uncommon, however, for Andarons to rob travelers.

"I'm addressing you," one man said. He rode a horse very much like his own, bare-chested with a scimitar sheathed over his shoulder and a bow at his saddle horn. The other warriors formed a half-circle around him – he clearly led them.

Eric didn't want to kill again.

"I heard you," he said.

He wasn't going to be pushed around, either.

"What are you doing here?" the Andaron demanded.

"Who are you to ask me?" Eric returned.

The warriors shifted on their saddles, looking at each other. One looked to the west, looking for his Millennia, most likely.

"My name is Uhanala Tladatis," he said. "I am chieftain of the Hunter tribe, and we are watching this army. We want to know what you're doing."

Eric nodded. "I'm traveling with them," he said, "but they're going to Chatoos. I don't know if I'm going that far."

Andarons had sorceresses among them, Eric knew. It wouldn't be smart to lie and get caught.

"Why not?" the Andaron asked him.

Now he was getting personal.

"It's the Emperor's army," he said. "I'm not necessarily sure I'm with them."

"You look Volkhydran to me," the Andaron said.

He nodded, but didn't say anything.

Let the other warrior do the talking, he knew. It's the smartest way to get him to tell you what he wants.

"I don't think I like the idea of Volkhydrans who side with the Emperor," he said, "so soon after the Emperor conquered their nation."

That was it, Eric knew. They'd fight. He meant to get himself a hostage, and Eric had just ridden into it, as fast as he could.

"No," someone said from behind the first rank of warriors.

She urged her mount out from between two warriors, a line of three behind her. Two of them carried spears at their sides, and one of them a staff, but the young girl leading them didn't have a weapon.

That wasn't her way.

"This one isn't with the Emperor," she said, looking into his eyes. "I know this warrior, and he's a friend of mine."

"Dagi..." the chieftain warned.

Dagi stopped her mount to his right and turned to look him in the eye. A young girl, she carried herself like a woman, with the confidence of a warrior.

"You sent us into that camp to find out what we could," she informed him, "and you agreed to trust us, Uha. Well, I found out that this warrior is a Volkhydran with his own mission, and he's with me."

The Andaron nodded. Dagi kicked her mount and walked him until he stood head-to-head with Eric's.

"Chesswaya says there's a reason we met, Volkhydran," Dagi said, "and Chessa's never wrong. I think you need to spend some time with my tribe for a while, and figure out your path."

Eric nodded. That sounded like sound advice.

Chapter Twenty:

Chatoos

On the 16th day of Water's month, the first of the Emperor's Millennia arrived outside of Chatoos and began to build their jess doonar.

Bells rang through the city, the gates closed, the city wharves shut down as Andarons and those visiting readied themselves for an attack by the most effective fighting force in Fovea. Lupus the Conqueror usually preferred to take his fighting to the plains, goading those inside of the city to come out and meet him, but the Andarons wouldn't be so foolish.

Eric watched them from on top of a low hill to the south, Dagi and Chesswaya on either side of him, Uha on Dagi's other side. For such a young girl, she commanded a great deal of respect from the warriors, and other than her forceful nature and her ready and often scathing opinions, Eric had yet to decipher why.

"He has to know they'll never come out to meet him," Uha said out loud. "The city dwellers hide behind their walls. They'll turn their toys around and fire rocks and spears, but they won't meet Lupus on the plains."

Their 'toys' were catapults and ballistae, perched on the outer walls facing Conflu. Their walls to the east and the south were significantly smaller and less well armed. It seemed to Eric that Vulpe would have been smarter to hold back his strength, gather a few daheeri to the east and then come on the city en masse, overwhelming it.

"We could sweep down right now and destroy them," another of the warriors commented. Dagi shook her head, just as Eric did.

"You'll meet their shields and their long pikes," she said. "They'll throw spears as soon as you get close, and you'll lose five hundred warriors before you even meet them. If we had ten strong tribes then we could meet them one-by-one, but our calls to the tribes have only brought seven, and most of those are small."

Most of the Andaron warriors were between here and Toor, trying their best to kill Swamp Devils and to collect their horns. The Emperor had promised one of Blizzard's scions to the first warrior or group of warriors who brought him ten pair of Swamp Devil horns, and every able warrior in southern Andoron had jumped on his horse.

Brilliant, Eric thought, shaking his head. He'd taken the biggest challenge to him and sent it away for its own greed. Not only that, but the Toorians were supposedly furious with the Andarons for invading their country to get to the Swamp Devils, and now *they* were useless as a resource to the Fovean High Council. Toor might have marched an army up into Andoron in a few months to aid the besieged cities, but they'd never do so now.

Whooping loudly, thirty warriors from one of those tribes flew out from the hills on their own initiative and made a run for the Millennia's supply train, firing arrows. Uha swore and sent one of his warriors to that tribe to tell them to stop doing that, and to the others to tell them not to follow. He might as well not have bothered.

A few Eldadorians fell to the Andaron arrows before a single command from the Eldadorian Major put the whole army into formation. Then thirty faced one thousand with pikes and shields. Arrows peppered the Eldadorian ranks with no effect. As soon as the Andarons closed, too brave or too foolish to break off their attack, a small flight of spears flew out and met them, skewering warriors and horses. Every man and beast of them were left screaming on the plains before a line of shields more than 1,000 feet long.

The Eldadorians remained braced for a second attack that didn't come, then broke apart and went back to their business.

Uha looked into Eric's eyes. "He's going to just leave them there?"

Eric nodded. "A message to you, Uhanala Tladatis," Eric informed him. "The Emperor has no mercy for fools and no quarter for enemies. Attack him at your peril."

Uha turned back to the plains and watched a horse with a spear through his belly try to stand, scream out in pain and falter. A warrior, pinned to the ground by a spear through his shoulder, tried to pull it out and couldn't.

"This man has to die," Uha said through grit teeth.

"As he would tell you," Eric said, "Plenty of warriors have looked him in the eye and said that, and they're all dead and he's not. If we want the Emperor's life, then we had better come up with a plan better than the one that he has, and if you want to do that, then you're going to need to know what his plan is."

"We can see what his plan is," Dagi said, pointing at the army. "He'll gather his strength, fifty thousand warriors strong, and he'll invade the city by force."

"The eastern walls are too weak," Uha said, and the warriors nodded. "Chatoos isn't prepared for an invasion from this side, not by foot troops. They'll take many lives, but they'll fail."

Eric shook his head. "No," he said. "If you know anything about the Emperor, then he doesn't just throw his warriors into arrow fire and spend them like coin. If he loses too many taking the city then he can't hold it when the Confluni come to take it away.

"No," Eric repeated. "There's a reason – the Emperor sent his son here, breaking out his army in waves, to give the Andarons in Chatoos plenty of time to be ready for him on this wall, and that means that this wall is the *last* place that he'll attack."

***

It would take five days for Vulpe to collect his Millennia outside of Chatoos. Ten arrived in the first, Nina among them, and Eric watched the people in the city scramble, tearing apart their defenses and moving them to the east and south.

To the north, they sent out their ships to ring the city. To the west, they sent scouts into Conflu. The Confluni were always jealous of their soil, however, and the Andarons were afraid to go too deep. It wasn't likely that the Emperor would fight Conflu *and* Andoron at the same time.

However, Eric considered, unlikely was the most likely thing for the Emperor to do.

Eric had watched Nina run out onto the plains, toward the watching tribes. She hadn't gotten near enough to see him, or at least Eric didn't think she had. It was hard to tell what those mystical gray eyes were capable of. He yearned for his woman in a way that he didn't think he could. Her hands in his hair, her lips on his face, her warmth against him. Nina had selflessly given of her heart to him, and Eric found that, as much as he'd tried to ignore it like a good Volkhydran male, it had become a part of him, and not having it was like missing a finger from his hand.

"You're thinking of your woman?" Dagi asked him, sitting her horse next to his, watching the Eldadorians.

Eric nodded. "Is it that obvious?"

Dagi chuckled. "She is the Emperor's woman more than she is yours," Dagi said, "But no one could doubt how she loves you. I saw it in her eyes the first time we met. If she'd thought that I wanted you for myself, then she'd have pulled her knives on me, I'm sure of it."

Eric chuckled. "And do you want me for yourself, Waya Daganogeda?" he asked her.

She chuckled and turned her head back to the city. "You're more trouble than you're worth," she said. "You can have your squirrel, if you can keep her. Most men find them too wild."

"Men say that Andaron wives are too wild," Eric said. "My grandfather told me that the reason that the Emperor conquers everything that he sees is because otherwise he has to go home to Shela."

"Ha!" Chesswaya laughed. She rarely spoke, so when she did, everyone usually paid attention to her. "Shela is almost always at the Emperor's side. She is terrified of losing him."

"As she should be," Uha said. He'd left them for a while, to rally the other tribes and see if anyone knew of a way to get more. "He reaches out his arm too long – it is going to come back a bloody stump one day."

"What news from the tribes?" Dagi demanded.

Uha shook his head. "None good," he said. "We've only two thousand – already we don't dare attack the Emperor's army. We've gotten word from Geeguh Digatish, Warlord of Chatoos, and he claims to have six thousand warriors inside the city now. He was expecting this attack eventually, but no one thought to warn him when this army landed. He was about to go to the Silent Isle, to hear the Emperor's man call for peace."

"Peace," Dagi spat on the ground, again more like a warrior herself than a woman. "Fine trick – he calls for peace as he attacks us. By the time they're done arguing, Andoron will be lost."

"He's sent a ship to the Silent Isle today," Uha told them, pulling his horse in between Eric and Dagi. "In a week's time, everyone will know that this is a trick."

"So he has to strike in a week," Eric said.

"Or he has to destroy the ship," Dagi countered. "Don't forget his navy is superior to ours as well."

Uha shook his head. "The ship will go to Conflu, and Geeguh's emissary will take a Confluni ship to the Silent Isle. Geeguh is no fool, much as he's a city dweller."

Eric nodded. The emissary had a good chance of getting through. They had a week before the Emperor struck, maybe less.

Another Millennia marched up over the horizon. It would probably not camp here today, but instead make a place a few hours from the city and come in tomorrow. Such precision, Eric thought. Like a machine – the parts ground through their motions, touching each other when they had to. His father had put this all together carefully in his mind, before he made it a reality.

Eric shook his head. "What in War's name is he planning?" he asked aloud.

Chapter Twenty-One:

By the Sword

For days, the Eldadorians filed into the plains to the East of Chatoos. Andarons madly rebuilt their city – tribes gathered on the plains, as many as five thousand strong. Uha had taken a commanding role among them, with other tribal chiefs and war lords.

Eric watched from his same hill, Dagi always to one side of him, Chesswaya always to the other. Nantar's daughters, Nanette and Thorna, always kept behind the other two girls, always with their spears ready, as if they'd decided that their role in life was to protect these two.

That bothered Eric on one level, but on another, it reminded him of Nina, and actually seemed to comfort him.

"With five thousand, we could take any single Millennia of the Emperor's army, but not two, and not if they were ready," Uha informed them.

"And they are," Dagi said. "More than once, a group of bucks have gotten together and made a run on their supplies, on their weapons, on their horses – the horses that *we* sold them."

"Nothing," Nanette chimed in. "You've accomplished nothing more than a few dead warriors."

"My father would tell you that you are wasting your time," Thorna said.

"An expression that he learned from the Emperor," Dagi said.

'My father,' Eric thought to himself, but said out loud, "We have to put a stop to that."

Eyes turned to him. He wasn't Andaron, he was Volkhydran. Some saw camaraderie between the races of Men, however this wasn't seen as clearly from *within* the races of Men, especially considering how easily the Emperor was perceived to have conquered Volkhydro.

"What do you see, Eric?" Dagi asked him.

He turned on his horse to face the girl.

"We learn among the tribes to *see*," she told him. "Look down the road, see your path, be on it, follow it. Most Men spend most of their lives trying to fight their way on and off their path – I want you to *see* yours, Eric. Look down your path, and tell me what you see."

The gem in the staff in Chessa's hand glowed green. She pointed it at Eric, and its light shined on him.

He looked down across the plains, across the enemy, and imagined that he could see a road, winding through it all.

"Look, Eric," Dagi told him. "Tell me what you see."

Eric saw the battle when it began. He saw the Eldadorians marshalling on the plains. He heard the trumpets and the drums. He heard the stomp that only Eldadorians made, the mathematical impossibility of thousands of feet striking the face of Earth at the exact same time.

He saw the missiles flying out from the city, crashing into the ground around the Eldadorians. But the Eldadorians wouldn't close, they wouldn't get within range of the missiles. They pressed the edge but wouldn't cross it – the Andarons thought that this was the Emperor's usual tactic, trying to draw them out onto the plains.

But that wasn't it – suddenly there was a ruckus behind the Andarons. Eric saw them falling, dying. Something was rolling up behind them, killing them, wiping them out. Something unexpected had taken them from the West – something that they never expected.

What? Eric strained to see – but that made the vision waver. In his mind, he heard Chesswaya telling him, "Be easy, Usdi Waya.

Don't fight it, don't reach for it. Let it come to you, and you shall have it."

Eric knew that 'Usdi' meant 'small,' or 'little,' and of course 'Waya' was 'Wolf.' The wolf was a prominent figure in his father's life. Perhaps he *was* the little wolf.

With that he imagined himself as a gray wolf cub, hiding under a stair in the city of Chatoos. He could feel his tongue loll, he could feel the fleas in his hide. He watched the Andarons, running past him, some falling. Usdi Waya could see arrows in their backs, the fletching, the shafts. He saw them falling, bleeding...

"No!" Eric shouted. His mount jumped – those around him as well. Dagi watched him with curious brown eyes, but it was Chessa's green eyes that he sought.

She knew. She'd gone there with him. He looked across the other horses, past the other warriors, at the girl with the glow dying out of her staff, and he knew that she *knew* his secret.

Chesswaya – Wolf Song.

Usdi Waya – Little Wolf.

Chessa knew who he was and, now, Eric knew who she was.

He wasn't alone.

"What did you see, Usdi?" she asked him.

He accepted the name. It was in the nature of the sisters of Andaron warriors to name their brothers – mothers would be too close. They could give children their names, but only a sister could know a brother well enough to give him his warrior name.

"I saw Andaron warriors running, not away from Eldadorians but toward them, toward the East, toward the enemy," Eric said. "I saw them fall with shafts in their backs, and I saw the shafts, and the fletching.

"And I know," Eric said, and he took a breath, looking around him. "I know that fletching from my woman's arrows. They think that the threat is here, like we do, but it's not. When he comes to strike, the Emperor has Aschire in the Confluni forest, and it's from there that the threat comes."

The Andarons all looked at each other, then at Dagi. How did she know, they probably wondered. How had a Volkhydran found his path like that? A million questions had to be running through their minds.

Only one ran through Eric's: How many brothers and sisters did he have?

***

"If we do nothing, then Chatoos will fall," Uha argued before the assembled chieftains. "And if Chatoos falls, then Talen falls right after."

"And what do we care, Uhanala Tladatis?" another of the war lords, Adahisdi Gádodi Hagata, demanded.

Eric knew this man – the war lord of the powerful Long Manes tribe. His name meant, "Kills with a Glance."

His daughter was the Empress Shela Mordetur.

"Will you be cut off from the Bay?" Adatlisai Kawi, Chieftain of the Proud Tail tribe, demanded. He was a younger warrior – barely twenty. He'd killed more than a dozen other warriors from various tribes, and his reputation held him so accurate with a bow and arrow that he could shoot an arrow in flight.

"What do I get from the Bay?" Adahisdi demanded. He was an older Andaron with gray streaks in his hair, and old, powerful muscles in his arms and chest. With a leather thong tied to either wrist, Adahisdi Gádodi Hagata could supposedly hold two horses running in two different directions.

Eric had a hard time imagining that any Man was that strong.

"The steel in your sword, the leather in your saddle," Uha argued. "Don't be a fool, Adahisdi – your son-in-law will strangle this land and very soon we'll have Eldadorian Dukes and Earls telling us what taxes we are to pay on our herds."

"My daughter," Adahisdi said, standing, "is an Andaron, and my *grandson*, Agtani Chewla, whose army you want to oppose, was raised Andaron, and they will *not* conquer the tribes."

"The Emperor," Eric said, standing, "could care less about your damn tribes. He wants power and land, and he'll take them where he can."

Adahisdi Gádodi Hagata waved a hand at Eric. "A stupid boy from a conquered nation," he said. "Ten Volkhydrans are no match for one Andaron."

"I'll do more than match you, old man," Eric said, and pulled his sword. The angry part of his brain raged now. "I'll gut you here and show you that ten of you aren't half the man as one of me."

Adahisdi Gádodi Hagata would never stand down from an insult like that. He leapt to his feet, his sword out.

Most of the chieftains and warlords just threw up their hands. If they were going to sit here and kill each other, then they might as well side with the Emperor.

The angry part of his brain told Eric that he needed to do more than kill a warlord here. If he just did that, then all he'd do is send one tribe packing until they could pick a new warlord. No, he needed the Long Manes.

He needed Adahisdi Gádodi Hagata alive.

Eric took a tight grip on his sword, he looked into the closing Andaron's eyes, and he said, "Strength to my sword – every word I have said today is true."

Adahisdi struck, swinging his scimitar wide, looked to hammer down on Eric's shoulder.

It was a feeling maneuver – a child could parry it. *How* Eric parried it would tell Adahisdi how well trained Eric was.

Rather than parry, however, Eric hammered back against the Andaron scimitar, putting his weight into the blow.

The scimitar shattered. Shards flew into the Andaron's naked breast.

Eric stepped back. Adahisdi held an empty pommel and crossguard, knowing that he should already be dead.

"Get another sword," Eric told him.

Adahisdi Gádodi Hagata looked at him, dumbfounded.

"Get another sword, you cursed Andaron swine!" Eric roared. Another chieftain stood and handed Adahisdi his sword.

"Strength to my sword," Eric said again, louder, so that everyone could hear, "Adahisdi Gádodi Hagata is thinking more about his relationship with the Emperor than he is about the tribes."

Eric closed on Adahisdi. The older warrior resisted giving ground, but instead made a half-hearted attempt at Eric's thigh. Again, Eric hammered down on the other sword with his own.

Again, the sword shattered.

Adahisdi Gádodi Hagata stepped back.

"Get another sword," Eric told him.

"You've made your –" another of the chieftains began.

But the angry part of Eric's mind was raging now, and its energy filled Eric's heart with red blood and bile. He swung the sword down on the log that he'd been sitting on, by the communal fire, and he chopped it in half.

"*Get another sword!*" Eric roared.

Another war lord stood – Eric recognized him as a member of the Sure Foot clan. This was a central clan to the Andaron plains – almost no clan didn't have a few in it, who could trace their roots back to the Sure Foot.

"This sword has been in my family for three generations," he said, handing the scimitar to Adahisdi. "It is blessed by Weather, and has never met its match."

Adahisdi took the scimitar and squared off on Eric.

Eric took his sword two-handed, the point touching the ground to his left, looking right into Adahisdi's eyes. "Strength to my sword," he said, again, "if Chatoos falls, then there will *be* no more Andoron."

He felt the power well from his own weapon. Adahisdi narrowed his eyes, took a step forward, and swung his sword parallel to the ground, coming right in on Eric's side.

Eric moved to parry, and Adahisdi pulled the strike. He spun the sword on his wrist and, as Eric's sword passed, struck for the boy's forearms.

Eric knew that move. He knelt, turned his wrists and bent the sword back. The Andaron scimitar met the black blade just inches away from Eric's forearms, then Eric flicked the blade away and rolled back onto his feet, catching the counter-strike from Adahisdi on his cross guard and then spinning it away.

Adahisdi chopped down at Eric's exposed thigh. Rather than moving, Eric chopped down on the offending blade. Normally, a move like that would have only driven the blade in deeper.

But this time, the blade shattered inches from his skin, prickling him with shards of steel.

"Impossible!" one chieftain said.

"No sword can do that," said another.

Eric straightened, panting. He let his blue eyes sweep the crowds of important Andarons.

"Anyone else want to test me?" Eric demanded of them.

No one said anything.

"Save Chatoos," he informed them, "or lose your way of life. You know the ways, you saw what you saw.

"You decide for yourself what's real."

Chapter Twenty-Two:

Clever, Clever

It didn't take the Andarons long to prove to themselves that there were, indeed, Aschire in the Confluni forests. No one but the Eldadorians knew the Aschire like the Andarons, and the Eldadorians had never needed to raid the Aschire for timber.

"If we know of them, they know of us," Adahisdi informed them, sitting on a log at the tribal fire where the chieftains and the war lords had gathered. Night had come at the end of a very busy day. More and more Eldadorians were gathering on the plains – their cook fires from the jess doonar lit the sky.

"We managed to find a few Confluni patrols," Adahisdi's younger son informed them. "The Confluni know of the Aschire, as well. They'll strengthen their patrol – they might drive out a few."

Eric shook his head. At sixteen years old, they considered him a senior advisor to their council now. They admired his sword and what they considered to be 'his magic,' little knowing that it all came from elsewhere, and that Eric, at least in his own mind, was just an adolescent trying to become a man.

He'd gifted Adahisdi, Uyosi Wagatsukanásdena of the Sure Foot Clan and the other war lord whose sword he'd broken with new scimitars. Uyo, an exceedingly fat Andaron with no hair, bragged of six wives and more than a dozen children, however all of them were daughters. Eric had joked that maybe he *needed* a new sword.

"The Aschire will stay clear of the Confluni, just like they stay clear of everyone else," Eric said. "I've seen Nina just disappear into the limbs of a tree. All they have to do is to stay hidden for two more days, and I don't think that the Confluni can have much more than a few more patrols in the area by then."

Already, Eric's mind was clicking out the steps in the battle. The Eldadorians would advance. The Andarons would ready themselves and start up a barrage from catapults and ballistae, rocks and long spears lancing out into the field. The Eldadorians would stop just at the edge of their range, and then the Aschire would sweep in from the west.

Natural archers and climbers, they'd be over the poorly defended western wall before the Andarons could react. Even warned, the Andarons would be hard pressed to defend themselves both from Aschire archers under the cover of Confluni trees, and fifty-thousand Eldadorian Regulars.

If the tribes could all be here, then there would be a chance. All that Chatoos would have to do would be to hold its own, and the tribes on fast horses would carve away at the supply lines and the outer Millennia of the Eldadorian army. They wouldn't have to win. They'd just have to make victory so expensive for the Empire that they would withdraw.

How to do that with so few riders?

There wasn't a warrior here who hadn't voiced the same question.

"Any luck getting word in to Chatoos?" Uyo asked, his lips greasy from a haunch he had been feeding on. Eric had never seen the man when he wasn't eating – his name meant 'Hungry Bull,' and whoever had thought of it knew him well.

Uha of the Hunters shook his head, his long, black mustachios waving. "None," he said. "There are too many Eldadorians now – they keep everyone and everything else out. We could send a message through the Confluni now, but it would take weeks."

"And we have days," Adahisdi said, leaning on the pommel of his new scimitar, its point in the dirt. "I love my son-in-law, I love my grandson, but today I curse them both, because they came up with this plan and they thought it out too well."

Eric turned to the west where, somewhere in the trees, he was sure someone from his woman's people was watching him, wondering what was going through these Andaron minds. They wouldn't expect a Volkhydran here – but then, what would they care? The Emperor had already defeated Volkhydro.

As he watched, a barge slipped lazily by. He'd asked about that, and been informed that there was some new city at the meeting of the Safe and the Great Mid Rivers, to the south, in Wolf Rider lands. Supplies were always floating down to it.

The Wolf Riders were the Emperor's Andaron tribe. Many had feared that *they* would come up from the south to hold the tribes, but they hadn't bothered. The Emperor more likely feared retaliation against *them*.

Eric saw a Man in the bow of the barge, poling it. There had to be others – no one could even steer a barge so big with one pole. The man wore Eldadorian green pants and no shirt, his huge biceps glistening in the hot sun.

"How can he be sending so many barges *and* fighting his war?" Eric asked aloud.

Oye laughed. "He isn't, Usdi," the chieftain said, laying down his haunch on his grease-stained thigh. "I thought the same thing, too, but in fact he only sends a few barges, and keeps them moving all the time. Then it *looks* like more barges, and we are supposed to think that he has great wealth flowing to the south."

One of the Andaron warlords, a tall, thin man with a bone through one ear, snorted and said, "Like we care if he buries rocks and gold in the south."

Eric straightened. Maybe they'd been looking in the wrong place for an answer to their problem. Maybe the answer to beating the Emperor lay with the Emperor himself?

"Adahisdi," Eric said, turning to the war lord, "how hard do you think it would be for you to capture a few of those barges?"

***

On the 21st day of Water, just as Eric had predicted, the Eldadorian army under the leadership of Prince Vulpe Mordetur, fifty-thousand strong, marshaled on the Andaron plains to the east of Chatoos. Their numbers spread more than a daheer wide and more than a daheer deep. The smell of their lancers' horses carried south across the plains. The smoke from the cook fires, all doused at once, obscured the sky.

Their trumpets deafened. Their drums shook the face of Earth.

Eric wore a horse-hide vest with padding underneath, and steel sleeves and leggings. He sat his excellent stallion with his half-sister, Chesswaya, on one side and Dagi on the other. Oye and Uha were his commanders in the field, and runners between them and him told them that all was ready.

'Wait,' the angry voice in his head told him, with surprising calm. 'Don't lose your advantage. When they're moving, they're at their most vulnerable – let them march, then strike.'

He nodded to himself. Chessa looked at the side of his face but said nothing.

Andarons were collected at the eastern walls of Chatoos. He could see the spearheads of the ballistae, pointed up for maximum range. Some would have light leads woven of horse tail attached to them – these would be drawn back, some with a screaming warrior attached. Others would be pulled tight to trip advancing soldiers. A few would have things like caltrops and walking stars attached to them with dung, to shake off between the enemy and the walls, to lame an advancing soldier in the field when they were stepped on. The Andarons had no intention of leaving their city, and so felt free to turn the plains around them into a hazard.

All of that worked well for Eric.

'Wait,' he heard in his mind. 'Wait.'

Suddenly the trumpet blare changed, and all blew one note, pure and clear. *That* would be the signal, Eric knew. Not just to the enemy to advance, but for the Aschire to be ready as well.

The Eldadorians started forward, all on the same foot. The ground shook at the impossibility of fifty-thousand right feet striking the ground at the exact same time.

They moved forward as one man, a beast under the control of the Prince of Eldador.

Now!

Eric didn't need to be told. He raised his hand. The runners ran.

Covering over four daheeri, bands of ten and twenty Andaron horse topped ridges, descended gullies, and exposed their numbers on the plains. Between them, women beat large kettle drums which the tribes used for dancing – boom-boom, boom-boom, boom-boom, *boom*! Over and over the ominous ringing of an enemy to the south.

But not just any enemy; the fierce Andaron tribes, come up from the south to save Chatoos! Tribes that numbered by the hundreds, and blooded warriors by the thousands.

Eric smiled – not really, but he'd learned from the Emperor. He'd spread the warriors out. He'd put them three deep in ranks, in groups of as few as five and as many as twenty. He'd had them move slowly, taking their time, as a huge army would, so that the front lines didn't get ahead of the back.

Vulpe had his orders, and Eric was pretty sure that this wasn't it.

Trumpets blew an alarm from the Eldadorians. The army immediately split itself into three pieces, one moving to the south to create a long line of shields and spears, another continuing to the city, a third staying in the middle between the two. Vulpe Mordetur wasn't sure what he was seeing, but he was absolutely sure that his army remained his best defense against it, arrayed defensively like this because the *real* offense came from the west.

Or so he thought.

"Send in the barges!" Eric shouted. More runners ran off.

Dagi grinned beside him.

They'd captured five of the Emperor's barges, overrunning the paltry guards and then beaching them down stream. Now they tied strong bulls to long lines and pulled them back up stream, much faster than a poling man could move them, older Andarons whipping the powerful aurochs into motion. The Andarons could care less right then *what* the Emperor's barges did and didn't bother them. Meanwhile the barges warded the aurochs from the Aschire archers on the other side of the river.

The river, of course, was the tripping point – how to get your one or two thousand Aschire across it? They could swim, but then they'd be scattered for daheeri on the other side, with wet arrows. They could be ported, but then you moved in barges like these and lost the element of surprise.

Or, as Eric had surmised, you could fell a great mass of trees and you could dump them at the mouth of the Safe River. They could come down as a group, and the Andarons, being the acrobats that they are, could skip across them. That would take a lot of trees, but then, Conflu *had* a lot of trees.

As the barges swept up the river, a flood of logs swept down. Aschire began to appear at the western water's edge, watching the logs, and watching the barges.

The Eldadorians pushed west on the plains, stopping just out of range of the city's ballistae and catapults. The Eldadorians formed a shield wall with pikes to the south, ready to meet the advance of the Andaron riders, scattered like a dark cloud across the plains.

The Aschire began leaping for the timbers in the water – if they could kill aurochs on the other side, then they could eliminate the threat that the barges presented, whatever that was.

Eric imagined that they probably got close enough to those barges to smell the oil that they'd been drenched in. Eric saw them stopping dead in their tracks on those timbers, the normally surprised-looking faces with the high, arched purple eyebrows looking even more surprised as they saw what they'd run into.

Eric didn't give the order – he didn't have to. Adahisdi was running that part of the front, and he was an experienced war lord. Suddenly the barges all exploded in flame, showering sparks down on the floating timbers. Most wouldn't burn – they'd had to float in Tren Bay for days - but they ran so close to the burning barges that nothing living could stay on them, and the effect didn't have to last forever. The barges, held in place by the aurochs with ropes affixed just above the water line, only needed to stay until the timbers passed. Even if the Aschire could get to the aurochs now, all they'd do is to turn a beast of burden into an anchor. The barges sat where they needed to be.

The Emperor's plan, laid so carefully, only needed a few moments' delay to fall apart.

Oye sent his riders into the plains, toward the gates of Chatoos, where they could inform Geeguh Digatish, Chatoos' warlord, of the Emperor's plans. Meanwhile Uha sent the gathered riders running to the east in a wide circle, cutting around the Millennia between him and the mainstay of the army, for the supply depot to their northeast. Cutting to the east of the Eldadorians' southern guard, peppering their troops with arrows as they ran, they forced the Eldadorians to build a defensive square and pinned them down, leaving their supplies wide open.

Vulpe sent the middle Millennia into motion to protect his supplies, but he couldn't out-race the swift Andarons. What the tribes couldn't just steal, they burned. They drove off a wealth of cattle to divide later, scorching a huge supply of vegetables and dumping gallons of water and milk on the ground. A flight of spears flew out from the middle Millennia but found few targets as the Andarons, having accomplished their goal, returned to their original places to the south among the hills and gullies.

Dagi laughed and clapped her hands. Chessa just smiled. Neither of them had expected *such* a success, Eric thought – he'd thought of everything. He'd outmaneuvered the cunning Emperor.

His father.

Vulpe's Millennia turned around. The supplies clearly couldn't be saved now. He'd come here to do a thing, and now there could be only one way to do it.

Vulpe would have to storm the city and, when he engaged, these warriors would harass his flanks and tear at his warriors. Now that the Andarons in Chatoos really *did* have only one side to defend, they could pin the Eldadorians down on the field, and they could last for days.

They could make this battle too expensive a win for the Eldadorian Emperor.

Eric had thought of *everything!*

"Well, well, my love," he heard behind him. "Haven't you found some quaint new friends?"

Eric turned to see Nina of the Aschire, with a dozen of her kind, standing with their bows drawn, a pile of dead Andarons between them and Eric, Chesswaya and Dagi. The look on her face told him that she knew who'd engineered this defeat for the Emperor.

The look on her face told him that he'd broken the heart of a dangerous woman, as well.

She raised a hand, white with power. To his right now, Chesswaya raised her staff.

Chapter Twenty-Three:

Father

The Aschire archers pulled their arrows back as one.

Then all the strings broke.

Nina struck for Chesswaya, white energy flying from her hand. Chesswaya caught it on her staff, held it, then launched it back at her. Nina flew backwards into her own warriors, the group of them scattering, then back on their feet in seconds.

Eric knew that he could slap his horse's behind and be gone from here, but he also knew that she'd bring down at least one of them. He'd just found this sister, and he wasn't willing to lose her.

He held his hand up. "Stop!"

Behind Nina and her kinsmen, two runners appeared, saw what was going on, and then left. There would be one hundred more Andarons here in minutes – then it would be a blood bath.

"You're taking us to Vulpe?" Eric asked her.

She smiled.

The angry part of Eric's brain raged. *Just kill her!* If he leapt at them, he'd likely come out the other side, and Chesswaya would back them.

He suppressed it. He knew better.

"Get on the back of my horse," he told her.

"I don't think you –" she began.

"*Move!*"

The normally-arched eyebrows arched even higher. Eric snapped his fingers, then jerked his thumb over his shoulder.

"I don't care what's happened," he told her, "you remember whose woman you are."

Her kinsmen exchanged glances, but she left her eyes on him. They almost glistened. She'd loved him, and those feelings don't just go away.

Not for someone who held them at bay for as long as Nina of the Aschire.

She came at him in a sprint. He held the stallion reined in. At the last moment, she leapt onto his stirrup, her foot as light as a feather on his instep, her hand on his shoulder as she spun around and seated herself behind him.

"To the base camp," she told her countrymen. They nodded as one and took off at a sprint across the battlefield, Eric behind them, Chesswaya and Dagi on either side.

He could have offered for her not to come, but in fact he knew she'd be going. He should have realized it when Nanette and Thorna weren't there, as they always were.

"Did you send them away?" he asked her, moving with his horse in the saddle, Nina with her arms around him.

"I told them that I needed them to go to the barges," she said. "I didn't think that the Andarons would do it right, and Nanette is *very* good with fire."

"Why?" Eric asked her, even though he knew the answer.

Chessa looked past him, to Dagi, then back to Eric. She looked forward, moving with her mount, the staff in her hand.

"I've been foreseeing this," she said, "and they didn't need to be here for it.

"This is for family."

Battle raged around them. A team of Andarons tried to pursue them into the Eldadorian army but had to break off when their casualties from spears cut their numbers in half. Eric would have expected Vulpe to be running with his own troops, leading among them, however the Aschire directed him to a blue and white striped pavilion in the middle of the army, past the southern defense line, and east of the Millennia that had already begun pressing Chatoos.

Nina leapt from the back of Eric's stallion. He dismounted behind her, Dagi and Chesswaya at the same time. No one made an attempt to take his weapon – they knew his status as a noble of Volkhydro and wouldn't try to disarm him except by combat or his surrender.

Dagi, on the other hand, kept no weapons, and no one in their right mind pressed an Andaron sorceress with a staff.

"Inside," Nina told him. The Aschire eyed the Wolf Soldier guards outside of the pavilion. Eric noted that Vulpe had added to their number – he didn't recognize these faces.

He stepped inside of the pavilion, Nina next to him and Chesswaya and Dagi behind. The place swarmed with warriors in armor, most of them with scarred faces, the Mark of the Conqueror which Wolf Soldiers considered the highest honor among them, a scar running from the corner of the eye to the jaw.

Activity centered around a long, low table. Eric saw chairs at either end, mugs on the corners of a long, wide parchment and wooden blocks representing troops on both sides of the conflict.

One figure dominated the scene – not a boy in toy armor and a short sword, but a full-grown man in shining steel, corrugated for more strength, over six feet tall, blond hair flowing past his shoulder.

He turned, revealing the piercing blue eyes and scarred face of Lupus the Conqueror. Rancor Mordetur, the Emperor of Eldador – considered the most powerful man not just on Fovea, but in history.

Eric's father.

Lupus' eyes searched Eric's face. Eric returned the stare. He'd never met this man, but he knew him, by his deeds, by his look, by the letters that he'd left Eric's mother.

"So this is the one who turned the battle for the Andarons," Lupus said.

"This is the one who thinks he has," his wife, Shela, said, stepping up from behind him. She wore the black leather skirt, harness and jacket of an Andaron raider. Black high-top boots laced up to her knees, a dagger in either side, and a harpoon in her hand.

The harpoon called to Eric more than the man. It almost sang to him – he felt a need to have it, to own it but, more than that – he knew that it didn't belong in the Empress' hands.

He looked to his side, to Chesswaya, and he could see the same feelings swimming in her eyes.

Lupus followed their gaze to the harpoon. He held his hand out for it and Shela handed it to him. He looking it up and down, feeling it for his balance, looking back at Eric.

"This?" Lupus asked him. "You come for this? All of this death, this unnecessary killing, for this stick?"

"You have a lot of nerve to complain of unnecessary killing," Dagi said, stepping forward. Eric put a hand on her shoulder but she shrugged him off. "You come here, you send your son, you create a war, you create a battle, for what? For more land? For more worshippers? How many does it take to fill the belly of the Eldadorian Empire?"

A smile crept across the Emperor's face. "The belly of the Eldadorian Empire," he said, "is *far* from full."

He dropped the spear on the ground, to bounce it on its end most likely, and it leapt from him, sailed across the room toward Dagi, landed in her hand.

Dagi – who'd never held a weapon in her life, pulled that spear to her like it belonged to her, and a part of Eric's brain told him that it did.

The Emperor pulled his own weapon - a long, shining sword, its edge gleaming - and held it in both hands. The room cleared, warriors in the pavilion stepping away both from the Imperial family and from Eric, Nina, Dagi and Chesswaya. Where the pavilion had been bustling with activity, now it sat quiet as a tomb.

Outside, the clash of steel on steel, the neighing horses, the march of warriors, told them that the battle raged despite them. It was the strength of the Emperor's armies that they could function without him.

"How did you do that?" Shela demanded. "I detected no magic."

"How did they do what, mother?" Eric heard, behind him. Vulpe pushed into the pavilion. More than likely, he'd seen them enter. He had his sword out, blood on it; blood splashed across his cuirass and breast plate and stained his greaves.

He'd been in battle – in the thick of it. Surrounded by his warriors, he'd taken his blood price again and again. Vulpe would prove himself as his father's son.

Eric could see that.

Vulpe stood right next to Eric. He looked first at the blond boy, then at his father, then back to Eric, then at his father.

Then to his mother, but Shela was already looking back and forth between Eric and Vulpe, between the two of them and her husband.

Between Eric and Chesswaya and Dagi, and Vulpe and her husband again. Her mouth dropped open and her hand flew to it.

"No," she said. Lupus turned to his wife and she stepped back from him.

"No," she repeated, and stepped away from all of them. "No, no, no, no, no."

"What?" Lupus insisted. His temper, Eric knew. That was supposed to be the Emperor's down falling. The Emperor was a force of nature – if you sent it in a certain direction, it would destroy everything in its path.

"Look at them, Yonega Waya," she said, pointing at the four children. "Look at their eyes, their noses, their thick bones."

Lupus turned and looked into their faces, the Andarons first, then at Vulpe, then at Eric, then at Vulpe.

Eric reached inside of his leather vest, and he pulled out the leather tube with the scrolls inside.

Lupus' eyes narrowed, then he smiled to himself. He looked into Eric's eyes and he asked, "Where did you get that?"

"My mother," Eric said. He opened it.

"I bore that scroll tube from the Great Dwarven Nation to the Fovean High Council," Lupus said. "I haven't seen it in more than a decade. When I was done with it, I threw it away."

"When you were done with it," Eric repeated, shaking the two scrolls out of the leather tube, "you threw it away. No wonder my mother wanted it."

He handed the scrolls to his father. He took them, and for a moment their finger tips touched.

Not rough, like a warrior. Soft, like a healer – that surprised Eric. The Emperor had soft hands, and yet who ruled with a harder hand than he?

Lupus read the full scroll, but he couldn't have gotten past the first few lines before he dropped it on the table and opened the second. He read that, too, and then he looked back into Eric's face.

"Aileen," he half-whispered, as if the word would call her like a dark spirit.

"My mother," Eric said. "Dead, and on her death bed, she gave me these.

"The only thing that she had left of my father."

Shela snatched the scrolls up. Dagi and Chesswaya took a half-step closer to him. Neither seemed surprised. Chesswaya already knew who he was, and most likely she had informed her sister.

His sister.

The daughter of the Emperor of Eldador.

But it was Vulpe who turned on him. "You have no claim," he informed his older brother.

Eric turned on him. "I didn't come here for a claim," he said. "I didn't come here for a throne in your stinking Empire. I came here for answers. I came here to know why *our father* left my mother to a life of disgrace and misery before she died."

"Aileen," Lupus said again. He turned to Shela.

Her eyes filled with hurt and anger.

That's when the pavilion flew up off of its posts, and the group of them found themselves surrounded by thundering Andaron riders.

Chapter Twenty-Four:

The Marks of a Legend

While the Emperor had been discovering his new found scions, the Andaron army had found a way around his southern Millennia and then made an attack directly on his central camp. Already his forward Millennia were back-pedaling to a more defensive perimeter to rescue him.

The Empress raised a hand white with power, her energy lancing out at the advancing Andarons. Chesswaya struck her with her staff, catching her completely unawares, sending her back forty feet into the ranks of the Eldadorians.

Lupus almost roared in his rage, sprinting off after her.

Vulpe shouted orders to his closest Generals, ordering the Millennia back to regroup and then push west. Eric stepped back from him, his hand on Dagi's waist, collecting her and Chessa. Their mounts had all run off, but it shouldn't be hard to catch others and be out of here.

Vulpe, like their father, was more than able to focus on more than one thing at a time. He leveled his bloody sword at Eric and shouted, "You!"

"I have no quarrel with you, brother," Eric said, but didn't sheath his own sword.

"I am *not* your brother," Vulpe spat back at him. "I have one sister living, and one sister dead, and that's all, Eric. That is *all*."

"You can't believe that, Chewee," Nina said, from behind Eric.

Eric kept his focus on Vulpe, but Nina pressed on. "Look at him, Vulpe – actually *look* at him. The eyes, the hair, the nose, the bone structure, the way he moves, the way he thinks – he's your father's son. He's more your father's son than you –"

That, Eric had to think, in retrospect, had been the wrong thing to say. It embodied everything that Vulpe had to fear, not just from a sibling, but from an older brother.

A brother whom his father might have loved before he met his mother.

Vulpe gave a younger version of his father's roar, a cub to a lion, and swung his sword at Eric. Eric parried once at the chest, again at the hip, and again at the thigh. The two swords crossed between the half-brothers, hilt to hilt, Eric the taller, the stronger and with a superior blade.

"You are *not* my brother," Vulpe insisted.

"You know that isn't true," Eric informed him.

Vulpe pushed away and struck again, faking for the thigh and going for the face – that blue eyed face, so much like his fathers.

Vulpe cut him from the jaw to the cheek, catching him on the point of his sword, Fury, opening that handsome face.

Vulpe stepped away, his hand to his mouth, looking into his brother's bleeding face, now wearing the Mark of the Conqueror.

Eric shook his head, throwing blood, spattering Nina and his sisters. If ever there had been a doubt, then it had to be gone then.

Eric was the spitting image of his father.

Vulpe roared again and cleaved his sword into the other's side. Eric caught Fury on his own sword's blade, hammering it aside.

The excellent short sword, forged by Dwarves as a present to their father on the birth of what they'd thought to be his first son, shattered.

Vulpe held the useless hilt up between them, looking into Eric's bleeding face, his blue, blue eyes, the tears running down his cheeks.

He threw the hilt at Eric, he turned on his heel and he ran. He might have been made into the Supreme Commander of the Eldadorian Regulars, but that didn't change the fact that he was still a thirteen-year-old boy, his sister had been killed, perhaps his mother, his father now had children other than he.

He wasn't the Emperor's only son anymore.

Eric took a step after him, but looked up instead and saw the Emperor, the Sword of War in his hand, and a look on his face that spoke of many things, but not the love of a father for a son.

"You!" he snarled.

"Your Imperial Majesty," Chesswaya began, but a look from him quieted her. He was focused on the son right now – he'd deal with the girls later.

"You're angry?" he demanded. "You think I did your mother wrong? You think it should have been you in the palace, you leading the Regulars? You want Vulpe's place? You think you're better than him?"

"I'm angry," Eric admitted. He began to circle to the left, his sword held low, the Emperor beginning to circle as well. "You did my mother wrong. I know you better now, I know what you were thinking, but you did her wrong, father."

Eric would have liked some reaction to the 'father,' but he didn't get it. The Emperor's sword stayed out. Eric didn't see Shela – he couldn't imagine what had happened to her, but it couldn't be good if the Emperor had stepped away from her.

His love for her was the stuff of legends.

"And the rest of it?" Lupus demanded.

Eric didn't even need to think about it. "I've travelled with Vulpe, I've seen what you're doing. I have no interest in it. Mother died a brewer – I suppose that I'm a brewer now, too. I'm perfectly happy being a brewer.

"All I ever wanted was a mother who was happy, and I never had it, and your greed is why, father. Your need to conquer. Your need to rule."

Lupus snorted. "You think I do what I do out of greed?" he demanded.

"You don't have the slightest idea."

Another troop of Andarons ran past them, Eldadorians throwing a flight of spears after them. The Millennia were reforming, the Andarons being moved back. Eldador would suffer terrible losses here, and not have the supplies to mount a siege. No matter what else he'd done, Eric of Myr – Eric Mordetur – had handed the Emperor his first, real defeat. He'd stopped Lupus the Conqueror from taking Chatoos – at least for today.

It was time to get the hell out of Andoron.

"Brother," he heard Chesswaya from behind him.

His eyes flickered for an instant in her direction, and the Emperor struck. Totally surprised, Eric parried, meeting the larger man with the heavier armor sword-for-sword, cleaving the air between them.

The blades met. The explosion that resulted sent Eric flying backwards at his two sisters, falling with them in a heap. Nina leapt clear, the Emperor flew back in the other directions, although not as far.

Eric shook his head. To his left Dagi shook her head as well, one eye blackened from his elbow. To his right, Chesswaya was making sure that her staff wasn't damaged, more concerned for it than for her own health.

He pushed himself up on his sword, his sisters on their staff and harpoon. Nina took a step toward him, then stopped, her mouth open, staring at his chest.

"War's beard," she swore.

"What?" Eric insisted.

The Emperor in heavy armor pushed himself over onto his stomach, got his knees and hands underneath him, and pushed himself up. He picked up his sword and took a step toward Eric, then stopped as well, staring at Eric's chest as if he'd been pole-axed.

"No," he said, much as Shela had a moment before. "No – no, that's impossible."

"What?" Eric demanded

"Eric, your chest," Nina informed him, pointing.

There, on his leather vest, in white, a hook symbol with a dot on top of it, emblazoned, almost glowing.

The mark of the Daff Kanaar.

www.ingramcontent.com/pod-product-compliance
Lightning Source LLC
Chambersburg PA
CBHW060424130626
46555CB00005B/2204